Shades of Difference

Rosalind Thomas-McCreary

authorHOUSE

AuthorHouse™
1663 Liberty Drive
Bloomington, IN 47403
www.authorhouse.com
Phone: 833-262-8899

Published by AuthorHouse 04/20/2021

ISBN: 978-1-6655-2333-2 (sc)
ISBN: 978-1-6655-2336-3 (e)

Prologue

While the two hundred fifty smiling graduates marched across the stage of Blue Keyes State College, Valery entered quietly through the doors of the second floor library knowing it would be empty. Walking purposefully past rows of tables and chairs, she found herself having gone as far as she could. She chose the chair that would free her. Breathing in deeply, she realized it would soon be the last time she would smell the combination of the dusty books and human scent that were eluding her thoughts. Already, she had begun to feel the warmth coursing through her body, caressing the thoughts that had haunted her. She could not change her fate nor did she wish to do so. Handily, she lifted the newspaper and began reading the headlines. When her body would be discovered, she hoped they would all face the truth. Finally, with ease, nothingness engulfed her senses allowing her to escape the struggle.

In the Beginning

Valery Lewis was ready to leave New York on the Greyhound bus headed for the campus of Blue Keyes State College in August of 1941 grateful that Mary, her older sister, had been named her legal guardian. After boarding the bus, she looked back one last time to see Mary's gentle face, urging her to be excited and to just think of all the possibilities that would happen in the years to come. The two of them had had a real heart to heart conversation the night before.

"Now don't worry." Mary had assured her. I've taken care of all the arrangements necessary for you to begin your first summer. I'll make sure you have spending change but remember not to spend it trying to look cute for some old boy."

Months earlier, their parents had been killed in an unfortunate car accident. Mary Lewis was twenty one years old then and Valery had just turned eighteen. Reeling from the emotional stress, they were determined to continue as if their parents were still alive. Mary took it upon herself to secure a secretarial job that provided food and shelter for the two of them until she could get her sister enrolled in college. The Department of Social Services for the state of New York had been carefully monitoring the whereabouts of Valery Lewis. She had an upcoming court date to determine through her case worker if her needs were being met. This time however was different since Valery was now an adult, she would no longer need to have Mary as her guardian. This would hopefully be the final hearing on the matter.

Twenty-five year old Toby Davis, a young white attorney, had been assigned to the Lewis case by the court. Valery and Mary had met with him several times at his office in Lower Manhattan. He was a rather nice man, medium statue, with a slight facial twitch. Valery figured it was probably just a habit he picked up from studying so much. Since it was difficult to come to his office with their limited transportation and funds, Attorney Davis had driven to their small row house in Harlem several times to help prepare them for the upcoming hearing.

Toby had never had a court case like this. As a matter of fact, he had only ever represented two other clients. His first two clients had committed misdemeanors, were both fined and let go. When Toby arrived at the small brownstone, Mary invited him inside and sat in the chair that had been reserved for their father. The house was immaculately clean and Toby was always impressed with the obvious care taken. Pictures of the family lined the walls of the living room. Above the fireplace were trophies and awards of both Mary and Valery during their time in school. Attorney Davis sat down on the couch and waited. In a moment Valery appeared. He stood and the two shook hands, exchanged pleasantries, and then began discussing how Mary should answer the questions he would ask.

When the court appearance day finally arrived, Mary was determined to do her best to convince the judge that she could provide the revenue Valerie needed to continue her education as a freshman in college. They arrived at the courthouse a few minutes after Attorney Davis and waited until they were let into courtroom. After the court case was called to session, Toby's first and only witness was Mary Lewis. When called, she stood, making her way past the creaky wooden floors, until she reached the witness stand. When asked, she raised her hand, swore to tell the truth and then sat softly in the large wooden chair just below the judge's bench. Toby Davis proceeded.

"Please state your name for the court." Toby Davis, dressed in a black suit, stood confidently even though he surmised his chances were just as close to losing as winning this case for the Mary and Valery.

"My name is Mary Lewis." She looked around the courtroom which seemed to be much larger than she had thought. Her voice echoed loudly bouncing off the walls and back to her own ears. Toby Davis continued.

"Thank you Miss Lewis. And what is your relationship to the defendant?

Mary looked lovingly at Valery remembering how life had been for the two of them when their parents were there. She wanted to become a lawyer before the accident but even more so now. But her dreams would have to be deferred a few years as it was extremely important that her sister attend and graduate from college. Mary had mapped the plans over and over in her mind. She would work to pay for Valery's college tuition and continue her education to become a lawyer later. Mary's educational awards and honors spoke for themselves. She was a great student in math and science, being the youngest to ever be inducted in the National Honor Society at Harlem High. Her first two years at NYU had been successful until the accident but she had to drop out leaving her future swaying in the balance. Her parents had been so proud of her many accomplishments but none of that mattered right now. She had little choice but to hope that the judge would grant her custody of Valery. She would get a high enough paying job or two that would help make her goals work to their advantage.

"She is my sister." Valery shyly smiled back.

"Do you currently reside in the same household?" Toby Davis wanted to establish that the girls had been inseparable, growing up together with two loving parents who had taught them proper behavior and had afforded them a good education thus far. He hoped that once he had established in the mind of the judge that Mary Lewis was indeed young but quite capable of providing the needed support and income for herself and her sister, he would be granted a favorable ruling.

"Yes." Mary almost wondered why Attorney Davis asked questions that he already knew the answer.

"Has there been a recent circumstance that changed the scope of your family and if so, could you explain?" He hated to put Mary through this line of questioning knowing it would bring back good and bad memories, but he had no choice.

After going over and over her testimony hundreds of times in her mind prior to today, Mary knew every word that she wanted and needed to say. But nothing had prepared her for the moment when she actually began to speak. As she looked down at Valery's face, a bit of her own mother glimpsed through reminding her of the last time they had been together. Starting with their childhood in the New York borough of Harlem, Mary vividly retold of their humble lives describing school, church life, and family trips. The car crash that ended her parent's lives somehow was etched into her mind like the last stitch of a quilt woven together. Mary fought back tears as Toby encouraged her to go on. The judge sat quietly and listened. At the end of the deposition, Judge Fiore ordered an hour recess.

Peter Fiore had been a youth court judge and was known in Harlem for his stern veneer and conservative handling of most cases presented him. He had served on the bench for over twenty years and had seen more than his share of cases involving children left without parents. In most cases children were placed in foster care until they were old enough to obtain employment and become independent citizens. The loss of parenting was different in this situation but the outcome was the same. Still there was something that bothered Judge Fiore about this case and it was nearly one o'clock before the judge reappeared to render his ruling.

"In light of the evidence that has been presented to me today, I would like to commend Miss Lewis for her testimony. It has been an unfortunate situation and I would like to personally extend my condolences to the both Miss Mary Lewis and Miss Valery Lewis."

Judge Fiore turned and looked directly at Mary who looked apprehensively at him. "I have reviewed this case and have thought a lot about the future of you both. I believe it to be unwise to grant custody of an eighteen year old to a twenty one year old that has meager finances and little more than a high school education."

Without waiting for Toby Davis to object, Mary rose and blurted out forgetting she was in the courtroom. "But your honor, I'll be twenty-two in a few days. I have a good job and a fine education with some training from NYU in law. I can take care of my sister if you'll just let me explain!" Toby, shocked by Mary's sudden boisterousness quickly stood and apologized to the judge for Mary's outburst and motioned for her to be seated.

"No. Let her speak. I would very much like to hear what Miss Lewis has to say."

"Your Honor, we loved our parents. Having lost both of them, we need your help. Now it is true that I had to leave NYU but because of the circumstance. However, my former roommate Jolene Brown contacted her father who recruits scholars to Blue Keyes State College, and he has offered Valery a scholarship to attend. Please give us the freedom to choose our destiny. Since Valery's GPA has qualified her for scholarship funding, her tuition, room, and board will automatically be paid. She can apply for work study there to pay for her books and I will send her as much pocket money as I can. I want the opportunity to make my parents dreams come true for both of us. Will you help me? Please, Your Honor"….

Judge Fiore had been humbled on this day. Having come from meager beginnings himself, he knew that had it not been for the support of key people in his neighborhood, he would not have been vested to judiciary status. Her selflessness had moved him. It took him exactly ten seconds to change his mind. Mary was awarded custody of Valery and life began anew for them both.

1

It was a warm sunny morning when the silver and blue-trimmed Greyhound bus began to pull away from the terminal. Even if Valery was awarded with full time work study, Mary knew that she would need nothing short of a miracle to keep everything going smoothly for the next four years. The two of them smiled and waved at each other as black smoke billowed from the exhaust encasing Mary's face, making her tears more plausible. The bus lumbered slowly into the traffic headed towards the turnpike.

It was the first time Valery had ever traveled such a long distance. The ride to Blue Keyes State College in West Virginia, was to take two days and she would travel it alone. The college recruiter, Dr. Cole Brown was to meet her at the bus terminal when she arrived in West Virginia. She had no idea what he would look like but her thoughts were flooded with the biggest challenge she had ever faced. Mary made sure she packed extra sandwiches for her sister to take with her on the bus since she didn't know whether Valery would run into any unkind souls that might say or do something to make trouble for her. Valery looked at her immediate surroundings to help her feel more comfortable about the journey that awaited her.

An elderly woman that looked to be in her early sixties sat beside her closest to the window. She appeared to have a pleasant countenance and her hair was speckled with some gray but it framed her face to enhance her golden colored skin. Seated across from her was a young man who was well dressed and obviously of military personnel. There had been much talk about the possibilities of war on the radio but she had hoped they were just rumors. She wondered where he was from and how he and his family had felt when he left his home. The man sitting beside the military man next to the window was obviously asleep and snoring so loudly that the military man cleared his throat in an attempt to awaken the man. Valery tried to smile inwardly as she settled in for her the ride to West Virginia. When the bus got quiet, she reached in her large satchel and pulled out a book to read. The first tear that brimmed her eyes was unnoticed by her riding partner, but a moment later the elderly woman without looking at her handed her a handkerchief. She was embarrassed but realized the lady probably had known she was trying to suppress her emotions all along. She accepted the handkerchief and wiped the tears from her eyes. Ten minutes later Valery gained her composure and opened the book she had taken out to read.

"What part of New York are you from?" The elderly lady asked never acknowledging the tears Valery had shed earlier.

"I'm from Harlem." She really wanted to be left alone but it would have been rude and so she tried to appear interested.

"I'm from the Bronx. I've lived there most of my life." She continued to talk. "Where you headed?"

"West Virginia." Valery had stopped thinking about Mary for a moment and started concentrating on what was being said to her. "And thank you for letting me use your handkerchief."

"You're welcome. I'm Eva Jones. Most people in the borough who know me call me Miss Eva. Don't worry, I've had to use one a couple of times myself."

Before long, Valery and Miss Eva though generations apart shared their lives with each other. Miss Eva, enjoyed inviting her friends to stop by her flat to have a cup of tea and some of her homemade biscuits with strawberry jam. She had one son and one daughter. Her son died before he turned two. Miss Eva never really knew why. She said the doctors thought it might have had something to do with a virus that he caught and her waiting too long to get him treatment. Her daughter was grown and lived in Greensboro, North Carolina. She had married a farming man eight years prior and they were about to have their second baby. Miss Eva was going to visit them and help out.

"I haven't seen my daughter very much. It's expensive to travel back and forth from New York to the Carolina's but this here was a real special occasion." She talked about how lucky her daughter was to have found such a nice man to marry. She remembered seeing the tall ears of corn that had grown on their farm. She was sure they would probably pick at least a dozen roasting ears for her to bring back with her when she returned to the Big Apple. Miss Eva told Valery about the last time she visited and her daughter had decided to ride their pet mule Pete.

"I'll never forget old Pete. He was a pretty good mule, just had a real stubborn streak in him at times. They were plowing up field to plant spring crops when Old Pete decided he was just too tired. Well, my little girl had always had a mind of her own so she decided she would teach him a lesson. She found a stick that was pretty thick and whacked him hard 'cross the head three or four times. That mule was so shocked that he took off before she could catch hold to the reins. She turned a backward flip and landed on her backside. It had rained that day and she landed right in the middle of a mud puddle. If you'd seen the look on her face because she then had to get up and run after Pete to get him to stop. White folks lived nearby and she didn't want to get in no trouble. Pete was her husband's favorite mule and she knew she'd have to do some tall talking if he found out that she had whacked his Old Pete about the head. Needless to say, she never bothered to try and boss Old Pete anymore." Miss Eva and Valery laughed for a long time and Valery listened happily as the bus rode along.

It was evening by the time they pulled into the Pennsylvania bus terminal for their first stop. When the bus driver turned the ignition off and opened the door, Valery was relieved. She made her way to the front and carefully stepped down the three steps. It felt good to stretch her legs

3

a bit. She stood just outside the bus looking around as the other passengers slowly woke up and exited too. They had a thirty minute break so she decided to go inside the station. There in the dimly lighted cinderblock building were several windows in which you could purchase tickets. She could see restroom signs down the narrow hallway. Across from the ticket counter was a small restaurant for purchasing sandwiches, donuts, and coffee. There were three wooden round tables with matching stools for customers who wanted to sit and eat the food they had bought. Valery passed the eating area but was drawn to the bubble gum machine she saw in the corner. She decided to buy one for herself but looked up when she heard the sound of the female waitress speaking to one of the bus riders.

"I'm sorry but you can't eat that in here." The waitress was talking softly to the elderly colored man that had been on the bus."

"But I bought it here." The waitress looked somewhat bewildered and tried to be diplomatic about the situation. She cast her eyes around to see if anyone of significance was looking or listening. She then lowered her voice even more.

"I think it's a silly rule too but if I let you sit down to eat your doughnut in here, I will lose my job. I'm sorry." The old man shook his head but got up and left the restaurant. As he steadied himself and began to walk away, Valery caught up with him hoping she could help him forget about the incident.

"Excuse me sir, do you have change for a quarter? I was going to buy some gum from the machine." The smell of the freshly baked donuts in the pastry case filled her nostrils as the man turned toward the voice that spoke to him. He looked irritated but changed his mind and dug deeply into his pocket with his free hand finding several coins. He really didn't have enough change but Valery decided to take it anyway. After buying the gum she boarded the bus offering a piece of gum to the gentleman who had given the coins. Knowing that she had witnessed the conversation with the waitress over the seat, he took the gum, offered a smile, and pushed the rest of the bagged doughnut in his pocket.

Once all passengers boarded the bus the big Greyhound was on its way. Miss Eva had reached the bus before Valery and had taken the window seat. She didn't mind and sat down beside her in the aisle seat. Miss Eva chatted on for another hour before she finally dozed off to sleep. Valery wasn't sleepy and let her mind wander.

Valery wasn't sure when she had fallen asleep but she awakened to the daylight dancing around her eyes and she inhaled deeply at the dawning of the new day. The young man who was sitting across from her had glanced over at least twice since she had awakened. Not knowing if she had slept quietly or snored half the night, Valery picked up the book she had laid on her lap before she fell asleep and began to read. After about an hour's time, the young man spoke.

"How's the book?"

"I just started reading it." Valery glancing quickly at him and then away. She was uncomfortable being friendly with males and especially those associated with the military.

"I'll bet it's a book about love and romance." The young soldier looked fondly at her.

"That's quite an assumption. I guess you think that because I'm female."

"Well, I guess that's part of it, but I had female classmates in school that liked to read books like that. Seemed like a waste of time to me but thought it was what most girls read about if they read at all." Valery could not believe her ears.

"I don't fit in that category either because the book I'm reading is about World War I. I did some studying about the war when I was in high school. History was one of my favorite subjects. I guess you know a lot about the war too."

"Not really. By the way, my name is John-Claude Adams. I noticed you when I first got on the bus. I'm from Brooklyn but I'm on my way to

Virginia. Actually, I was drafted by the military. I'm headed to boot camp training in Virginia. Guess I'll be reporting for active duty soon enough." Valery could tell that even though this man looked strong and confident, there was a meekness about him that made him seem vulnerable. She wondered if he was afraid that once he left the shores of the United States he may never come back. She ventured to keep the conversation going.

"Does the thought of war bother you?" She figured he would say no but since most of the people on the bus were still asleep he might reveal his true feelings about the whole situation to her. Maybe she would reveal her true feelings about her situation too.

"Well, sort of, but not really. I look at it like this. My only real knowledge of the war is what I've read, but if going will save my family and the people I care about from danger, I'm all for it."

"You mean you're going to fight for a cause and you don't know what it is?"

"Oh, don't get me wrong. I know the real reason is that every major country wants to control the world." As John-Claude continued he leaned into the aisle and lowered his voice. "When the letter from the draft board came, my mom was so upset. She cried a lot. Some of my classmates that received letters ran away from home hoping they would not be found. I knew I could never be a draft dodger even before I got the news that I was being drafted. I figured that if the good Lord decides to call me home, war or no war will stop that.

"I guess you're right." Valery was tempted to tell him all about the war. She had studied it in history class and enjoyed reading about it. She could just see it all taking place. It really all started with the First World War. In the end, the United States, France, and Great Britain were the three countries that were satisfied with how it turned out. Valery remembered a report she wrote in her history class about it. Japan didn't get control of the land they wanted, Italy didn't gain enough land or satisfy its ambitions and Germany was angry because it didn't feel that it should have had to pay for the damages it caused through the Treaty of Versailles. Valery, however, was afraid she would sound like a show off so she didn't bother to say anything.

John-Claude righted himself in his seat and waited a few minutes before he attempted to continue the conversation he had begun with Valery.

"So, you're on your way to college."

"Yes. I'm going to try it for the summer and if I like it, I'll come back for the fall semester." She smiled inside trying to sound as if she had lots of choices. John-Claude was amused.

"What's your favorite subject?"

"I don't really have one. I like lots of things, but I mostly enjoy sports. I was the captain of my school's basketball team and well, I guess I excelled in most sports. If I have my way though, I think I'll become a physical education teacher. That way whatever I decide to do, I can share all I know with students. "

"You sound like you know what you want. I'm sure you'll be a fine teacher one day." John-Claude didn't tell Valery that she was talking to a teacher who not only loved his profession, but also hated that he was having to give it up for a cause so foreign to him. The ride went on for hours until finally the bus driver announced that he had reached Norfolk, Virginia and all passengers would need to find their connecting buses. After exiting the bus, Valery shielded her eyes against the bright sun that loomed overhead. When the storage doors were open, Valery quickly spotted her bag and was one of the first to retrieve her luggage. She lingered for a moment to say goodbye to Miss Eva and John-Claude.

2

On Saturday afternoon, Valery arrived at the Marigold bus terminal in West Virginia. Her legs were tired from sitting on the bus and she rubbed her stiffened neck. She longed for a hot bath, clean clothes and some food when she heard her name being called. Although the ticket line was already full of other passengers trying to get their tickets, Valery approached the window clerk setting her two bags in front of her.

"Yes ma'am. I am Valery Lewis." The clerk hardly looked up from the ticket counter.

"A Professor Cole Brown from Blue Keyes State College should be right outside there." The clerk pointed in the direction of the farthest exit door.

"Thank you." Valery picked up her bags and had only walked only a few feet before once again her name was called.

"Miss Lewis?"

"Yes. I am Valery Lewis." Valery was not used to being called Miss Lewis but she knew that as a potential college student, she would be addressed as a lady and she would have to get used to it. The face in which Valery stared was a tall, well-dressed, medium brown skinned man with chiseled features.

"I'm Professor Cole Brown from Blue Keyes State College." He shook Valery's hand wanting to make her feel at ease. He could tell by her sweaty palms that she was a bit reserved but he knew that was to be expected given it was her first time away from home. To boot, she would soon be living in his home with this wife, at least for the summer.

"I've heard wonderful things about you and I'm so glad to meet you. My car is parked right around the corner. Let's get your luggage and we'll be on our way."

Valery had not known what to expect but his mannerisms had already starting making her feel welcomed. Cole Brown was tall in statue and seemed to command a distinction that made her feel special.

"I'm sure that you could use a bit of freshening up and a good hot meal to start with. My wife has been cooking all day. She's known around the campus for cooking delicious meals. I hope you're not disappointed."

"Yes sir." Valery was glad she had arrived in West Virginia and was getting closer to her destination.

The day was beautiful and she winced as she looked into the bright sunshine. She followed Professor Brown and watched him load her bags in the trunk of his car. He was a perfect gentleman, opening the car door for her and waiting for her to settle comfortably before closing it. He slid in on his side, started up the ignition of his 1939 Ford Tudor Sedan and quickly joined the traffic headed to Blue Keyes State College.

"Have you ever been to West Virginia before?" Cole knew that she hadn't but he needed to get Valery to talk about something to pass the time until they reached campus.

"No. But I remember reading about the Hatfield's and the McCoy's. I believe they were related to each other and somehow got into some kind of land dispute.

"I hope you don't hold that against us." Cole Brown laughed as Valery wondered if she had missed something. He hummed as he continued to drive down the road leaving her the luxury of viewing the mountainside undisturbed. Valery's eyes darted from side to side taking in the grandeur of the blue ridged skyline.

"So this is West Virginia." Valery thought silently as she saw houses that seemed to just stick out from the sides of the hills. She noticed there weren't many cars on the road in comparison to the busy streets of New York. He seemed to have read her mind as they drove on toward the college.

"You're probably wondering what happened to all the traffic."

"It's just that I'm used to seeing lots of people and traffic everywhere but it's so peaceful and calm here. I'm sure I'll get used to it."

Blue Keyes State College was located twenty miles south of Marigold, West Virginia. Professor Brown explained as much as he could to her as they drove the highway passing the Kanawha River. Valery was in awe of how this place seemed to be so picturesque with the mountains, taller than New York skyscrapers. As a matter of fact, there weren't any tall buildings. The Brown's family lived on the campus in a small white fenced cottage. Since Cole Brown's daughter Jolene had left to pursue her education in New York and was Mary's roommate before her parents' accident, there was no one for his wife to pamper so she was looking forward to Valery being their summer guest.

As they pulled into the graveled driveway, Mrs. Brown came out to meet them. She was a short, pleasant looking woman with a round face and a wide smile that immediately made you feel right at home.

"Hello there. I'm Mae Belle Brown and you must be Valery." It proved to be a wonderful afternoon. She offered Valery the bathroom facilities while she set the dinner table. The dinner was divine with roast beef, green beans, pickled beets, potato salad, rolls and chocolate cake for dessert. Valery couldn't believe all that had been done for her. After helping Mrs. Brown clear the table, she was shown to her room and went to bed early that night.

Before she went to sleep she remembered to do two things. Using the notepaper she had brought with her, she sat down and composed a short letter to her sister. There was no telephone in her bedroom and even if there had been one, she would not have had money to pay for an out of state call. After she finished, she crawled into bed and silently prayed the prayer her mother and she said recited each night from her childhood. It was the last thing she remembered before falling asleep.

The next morning there was a quiet knock on her bedroom door. It was the voice of Mae Belle Brown calling her.

"Good morning dear. I hope you slept well. It's time to wake up and get ready for your first day on the campus." Valery was awake and had been thinking about the day since early that morning.

"Oh, please come in Mrs. Brown."

"I just wanted you to know that when you finish your bath and are ready to have breakfast, come on down. I hope you like French toast and bacon."

"Oh yes. That sounds wonderful."

At breakfast, Mrs. Brown told Valery that her husband had left for work earlier and that she would show her around the campus whenever she wanted. Cole Brown thought it would be more appropriate for Valery to be seen with his wife as a guest in their home before he introduced her as a potential student at Blue Keyes State College. Mrs. Brown and Valery left the small cottage around 9:30 a.m. and toured the campus on foot. They began with the dormitories for women that included Frazier, Douglas, and Waters Hall. Frazier Hall was strictly for freshman. Douglas Hall was for sophomores and juniors, and Waters Hall was for female upperclassmen. Valery looked at Frazier Hall with great intensity knowing she would stay there in the fall if she returned. Mrs. Brown also pointed out the male dorms. Welch Hall, Ballard Hall, and Livingston Hall were the dorms for the males. The cafeteria was located midway the campus and the academic buildings were on the East end of the campus, along with the physical education building. The business offices were on the west end of the campus. The library was located in the administration building. The infirmary for students was located in McCommas Hall. There were two doctors and two nurses on campus at all times and the nearest hospital was within a ten-mile radius. When the two had finished walking around the campus, Mrs. Brown took Valery to Professor Brown's office located on the second floor in the business office. Mae Belle knocked lightly on the door.

"Come in." Cole Brown and one his colleagues rose at the sight of the two women as they entered the room.

"I'm so glad that you're here. Dean Gilbert, I believe you've met my wife Mae Belle and this is a new hopeful from New York, Miss Valery Lewis." Valery extended her hand and the two were invited to sit. Mrs. Brown declined but left Valery there promising to see her back at the cottage later in the afternoon for lunch. Professor Brown focused the conversation on the three of them.

"Miss Lewis, Dean Gilbert is the head of Student Affairs here at the college and he's delighted that you are considering attending Blue Keyes State College. I'm going to let the two of you talk. I have a class to teach in a few minutes. When you are finished, please feel free to walk around and I'll meet you back here at my office say in about an hour."

Once Professor Brown left, Valery felt a little nervous but she tried not to show it. George Gilbert asked her questions about her background and her career goals. He shared the college's philosophy of education and told her about his family. She asked what his job was like and he eagerly shared his job details with her. When the two of them left Mr. Brown's office, he walked her down the hall to meet Mrs. Harris, one of the freshman advisors. Dean Gilbert asked her to go over the general freshman schedule with Valery and to acquaint her with the expectations of a freshman student.

"Welcome to Blue Keyes State, Valery." I'm sure this place looks rather small to you, taken that you come from such large population.

"Yes. But I really think this is a very special part of the country. The mountains are so beautiful."

"You should see them in late fall when the leaves turn. You would really appreciate the beauty then. Now let's see. Mrs. Harris shuffled some papers around and cleared a little space on her desk. She reached among her many books and pulled out a college catalog.

"What are you going to major in dear?"

"I really hadn't decided yet. I think my physical abilities are my greatest asset." Valery was indeed well built. Mrs. Harris smiled as she gazed at Valery's lovely frame. With the exception of her dark complexion, she would fit in well at Blue Keyes State.

"I'll tell you what we'll do. Let's just assume you chose physical education as your major. That's about eighteen hours per semester. Then you'd have to put in a few extra hours for your student teaching and finally take your comprehensive exams before graduation." That sounded like a lot to do but Valery was sure that she could do it.

"How will I know which classes to take and when to take them? She talked freely to Mrs. Harris who seemed to enjoy talking candidly to her.

"I'll give you a catalog listing of all your required course work. You have the option of selecting the actual classes you take. It's always good to work with your advisor so the two of you agree that you're on the right track and taking the right classes. Other than that you're ready to go. Mrs. Harris noticed Valery glance at the large clock on her office wall.

"And by the way, I think you will enjoy the relaxed atmosphere that Blue Keyes has to offer. You will get a chance to meet a lot of different people. The students that attend here are not just from this region, but are like you, from all across the United States. You'll learn to adapt to each other. If you have any problems, you can always seek counseling or help from your advisor. There are several freshman advisors and one will be assigned to you if you decide to return in the fall. Is there anything else I can do to help you right now?"

"No. Thank you so much for sharing your time with me. I think I'm beginning to like the idea of coming to Blue Keyes State. Should I return the catalog to you after I decide on my major?"

"It's yours to keep." Mrs. Harris liked Valery's personality. She thought

Valery seemed to be a little reserved but was sure that once she mingled with other students, things would be all right for her. The only problem she could foresee for Valery was the darkness of her skin. Girls that were fair skinned and had longer hair were generally given more breaks but a good personality would count for something.

It was almost noon when Valery saw Professor Brown again. He had just finished his last morning class. The two walked down the hall to the front door. He looked at his watch and guessed that Mae Belle would have lunch ready by the time the two of them made it there. The walk back to the Brown's cottage gave Valery a chance to tell him everything that Dean Gilbert, Mrs. Harris, and she had discussed. He was glad her first encounter had been an enjoyable one. As they neared the cottage, Valery spotted Mrs. Brown picking daisies from the small garden patch in the front yard. She waved and the three went inside.

"Hey babe." Cole Brown kissed his wife and then turned to Valery. "If the food on the stove tastes as wonderful as it smells, we're in for a real treat." It hadn't been since the death of her parents that she'd felt a real family environment. She realized how she longed for it.

"May I help you with anything Mrs. Brown?"

"Sweet of you to ask but there's really nothing to do. I hate to admit it but my daughter Jolene and my husband are a bit spoiled. He enjoys hot meals and doesn't eat many leftovers. I usually cook three times a day so this is really nothing special." She moved around her kitchen with ease as she added sugar to the lemonade without measuring.

"If you could reach up in that first cabinet there and get three glasses down and fill them with ice it would be a big help."

It began that way for Valery in the Brown's cottage home. After a while, she learned her way around. Over the next month, Valery began to feel like a family member. Mae Belle enjoyed Valery's help in the kitchen, her folding and ironing clothes and offering to help out since Jolene had decided to stay in New York for the summer. Professor Brown was able to secure a temporary job for Valery on campus to pay for the two summer classes she took. She was assigned to the administration office where she would run errands for the second floor secretaries. If they needed information picked up or delivered from one office to another Valery took care of it. After her first week of getting to know everybody, she found her way around and the people she worked with liked her a lot. She would even go to the cafeteria and pick up lunches for the secretaries who had heavy workloads and couldn't stop to eat lunch. She watched everything that came and went on the second floor of the administration building. She felt that what she did to help was really nothing considering the fact that she was living in a lovely cottage with a college professor and his wife. The college was beginning to really feel like home to her and two weeks before the summer was over, she made her decision. She knew it would be a struggle not having her sister with her, but realized she could actually help Mary by not being more of a financial burden to her. If she could get a good part time job and her scholarship was funded in the fall, she would not have to ask Mary to send her money. It was a perfect solution to the problem. The next morning Valery shared it with the Brown's.

"I've decided to enroll at Blue Keyes State in the fall." Valery said it casually not wanting to seem overly excited about it, especially since she thought that was what they had expected her to do. Professor Brown had just passed the platter of pancakes to Valery when she made her announcement. Mae Belle jumped up from the table in her usual bouncy form and kissed Valery on both cheeks.

"I just don't know what I would have done if you wouldn't have decided to stay. I told Cole I knew that summer would be over soon and I guessed you'd be going back to New York for good since you hadn't mentioned it. I couldn't be happier." Cole Brown smiled broadly. "I think you've made a wise decision young lady." Valery knew that if for no other reason he had to be proud that his recruitment efforts had paid off.

For the rest of the summer semester, with help from Professor Brown and advice from the secretaries on the second floor of the administration building, Valery began making plans. Since she was there long before the fall semester began, she was allowed to choose her room in Frazier Hall. Deciding to stay on the ground floor close to the matron's quarters, she hoped to be of some assistance to them since housing was as important as anything else. Besides, she knew she'd need quiet time to study. She had been told that only the "brainstorms" would want to be near the matrons.

One late summer evening after dinner, Valery went to her room to look more closely at the course catalog Mrs. Harris had given her. She would major in physical education and minor in biology. Her mind drifted to post graduation as she imagined herself a well-respected leader in the field of physical education. Maybe she would become a physical trainer for college athletes or more importantly be on the front lines of advocating physical education in schools all over the country. She could see millions of people being able to live healthier and longer lives . She also could imagine herself with Mary acknowledging the accolades they both would be blessed to have once Mary reentered and graduated from NYU as a lawyer. Perhaps she would use her agility to become one of the great athletes to represent the United States in the Olympics. She would swim or run or jump faster and farther than anyone and win gold medals for America, bringing pride to her family and to Blue Keyes State College.

"Valery…Valery…Valery?" Valery wondered how long Mrs. Brown had been standing in the doorway of her room.

"I'm sorry Mrs. Brown. I must have been daydreaming." They both smiled and giggled out loud.

Soon, the summer school session had ended and it was time for Valery to return to New York. She was thrilled at the thought of seeing her sister again since they had only been able to write letters to each other. She would miss Mae Belle Brown and the wonderful meals she cooked while in her care. When she returned in the fall she would not be allowed to stay with the Brown's but she could visit as often as she had time. Mae Belle held back her emotions as Valery opened the passenger side of the Ford Sedan and shut the door.

"Please let us know if there's anything we can do for you Valery. You are always welcomed to stop by when you get back. You have been like a daughter to us. Please don't be a stranger."

"I won't. I can't thank you and Professor Brown enough." Valery could already smell the freshly baked cookies and sandwiches she prepared for her bus ride back to New York. Cole Brown loaded Valery's bags and started the engine. As he backed out of the graveled driveway, Valery waved one more goodbye to Mae Belle Brown as Mr. Brown started toward the bus station.

3

July was always such a wonderful time of year in New York. Tourists flocked to the city for first hand visits to see the Statue of Liberty, the Empire State Building, and Manhattan Park while enjoying the warm daytime temperatures and cool evenings. Mary found herself thinking constantly about being the sole financial provider for her younger sister and herself. Thankfully, with the country gearing up for war, women were being recruited for jobs normally given to men. Because of defense employment and the draft, women found employment as service station attendants, cashiers, streetcar conductors and even street sweepers. She had been fortunate to have been hired by Macy's Department Store. The store was one of the largest in the world.

On Saturday, July 12, Jolene Brown had driven by to visit Mary and offered to pick Valery up from the bus terminal in New York. They found the closest parking space and jumped out quickly to find her. Mary thought it would be a great idea for Valery to meet the person that was really responsible for her getting to Blue Keyes State College. It was through meeting Jolene at NYU that the scholarship had been made possible for Valery to attend. Without the first word spoken, Valery could tell right away that Jolene was the daughter of Cole and Mae Belle Brown. She had Mrs. Brown's smile and Professor Brown's physique. The two sisters hugged each other tightly, rocking side to side emitting a braved silence that said more than any words could have. Mary introduced Jolene and the three quickly loaded the car and never stopped talking until they got to their brownstone. Once there, Mary and Jolene helped Valery carry her things to her room. She decided to unpack later since they had mounds of catching up to do.

"What's the surprise?" Valery was pointedly curious.

"First things first little sister." Mary insisted. "We're going out on the town."

"I'm kind of tired from the trip Mary. Besides, my clothes are all probably wrinkled." Truth told, Valery wasn't tired but didn't have any nice clothes to wear. Mary and Jolene disappeared into Mary's room and in a moment reappeared holding the most beautiful sky blue cotton shift dress she'd ever seen.

"Try this on for size." Valery let out one of her rare squeals much to the delight of Mary and Jolene and before long you would have thought all three of them were sisters. The girls, in their pastel dresses and low heels, all hopped in Jolene's car and headed down the street taking in the sights, smells and sounds of Harlem.

"Thank you so much Jolene. I had a wonderful summer with your parents."

"They said the same thing about you. By the way, do you think you might go back in the fall?"

"Yes. Mary and I wrote each other during the summer and she agrees that it would be a great place to study, get my degree and enjoy the experience of college life."

Valery had never been to the Savoy Ballroom and the lines were long.

"Let's stay close to each other until we get inside and find a table." Twenty minutes later the girls were seated listening to the beautiful sounds of Coleman Hawkins and watching the intricate footwork of the lindy hop and jitterbug by neighborhood swing dance couples. Valery's eyes were glued to the dance floor and their intricate footwork. The girls ordered soft drinks and enjoyed the dancing and entertainment long into the night. The smell of thick cigarette smoke made the girls want to leave but not before they found a pen and had Mr. Hawkins autograph their napkins. When the evening ended, they drove home and talked into the wee hours of the morning.

Mary had just come out of the bathroom with her robe wrapped around her.

"Good morning, Valery." She slowly opened her eyes and rubbed them remembering she was in New York with her sister. She didn't want to miss anything so she slept on the couch.

"Did you sleep well?"

"Oh yes." The excitement of being with her sister and taking in a bit of Harlem was like taking a sedative. She had almost forgotten how busy the city was. Valery swung her curvaceous legs and repositioned her hips to an upright position.

"Where's Jolene?"

"She left earlier this morning. She's on her way to visit her folks. She told me not to wake you since you were sleeping so soundly. She'll be back in a week and will stop by when she returns. In the meantime, we'll find something to do. Go take your bath and get dressed kiddo." It wouldn't take Valery long to get ready. She hung the three skirts she owned on wire racks behind the bathroom door trying to decide which one to wear.

"Are we going somewhere special today?" Valery yelled from the bathroom.

"I thought I'd take you to Macy's so you can see what I do for a living. There are some really nice people there and I think in the near future I just may get a promotion. My boss, Miss Sandy says I have a way with customers. They trust me and usually customers buy items I suggest. When they're complimented, they come back again and again. Sometimes when I'm go out for lunch, a customer will come in and ask for me by name. If I'm not in, they leave and promise to come back when I return."

"That sounds great. You always were the one who could get people to listen to you."

"Just wait until you meet Miss Sandy. You'll like her." Sandy Murphy, manager of Macy's department store had given Mary the go ahead last week to help a long time client plan her daughter's trousseau. She could tell that the woman was of means however, the pieces that Mary helped her choose were not only expensive but in such good taste that the client gave her a big tip afterwards. Miss Sandy told Mary that with her skills, she'd probably open her own clothing shop one day.

"So you really enjoy your job?" Valery realized the sacrifice her sister was making for her.

"I guess so. Are you ready?" The girls left the apartment, caught the subway headed to 151 West 34th Street. Once they made it to the street, they weaved through congested sidewalks, walking for several blocks until they reached the well-known department store. When they arrived Mary took Valery to her boss's office and introduced her to Miss Sandy. Mary had arranged to work until noon in order to spend the rest of the day with her sister. She had to take advantage of their time together. Valery would be leaving in two weeks to begin her studies back at Blue Keyes State.

There had been a steady stream of customers coming and going that morning. Tourists were always looking for little souvenirs to take home from vacationing in the Big Apple. Mary always took time with customers who were looking for such items because it seemed just as important to provide customer service for those who had limited funds with the hopes they would tell others where to find great affordable gifts. Bracelets with dangling trinkets, broaches, pearl earrings, scarves, and monogrammed handkerchiefs were always popular. As the time neared noon, Mary glanced at her watch. She hurried up the escalator toward the office to sign out but slowed her pace as she could not help but overhear familiar voices.

"Can you believe that girl is Mary's sister?"

"Her skin is so much darker."

"They must have had different fathers or mothers."

"Or maybe she fell into an ink well." The snickers had now turned into full blown laughter becoming louder with each slur made. As Mary entered the room, the sales girls cut their eyes in her direction and then all found reasons to need to get back to work. They acted as if they had said nothing. Moreover, it didn't matter to them one way or the other. They were Caucasian and would not be in danger of losing their jobs. Her first impulse was to confront them but feared it might make the situation worse. She couldn't afford to lose her job over the matter. Valery would never know what had been said and she'd pretend she didn't hear it. No one would be the wiser. She picked up the pen on the desk and signed out. She would let nothing spoil her day or the few weeks she had to spend with her sister.

4

Jolene Brown had driven to West Virginia from New York hoping to surprise her parents. Professor Brown had bought her a used car that was in mint condition. It was a gray 1935 Ford with off white interior. Professor Brown wanted to make sure that his daughter had reliable transportation wherever she went. This would be Jolene's first long distance trip. She knew that her parents would not have approved of her driving alone so she didn't tell them of her plans. She had hoped Mary would be able to come too but since Valery was in New York, they needed to spend time together so she decided to brave it alone. It took several tanks of gas to get there and the only thing she worried about was the possibility of having a flat tire. She had her car serviced in the automotive department at New York University before she left. It was nearly one o'clock the next afternoon when she arrived at her parent's cottage. She honked her horn and Mrs. Brown came to the door. When she saw her daughter's face she unloosened the tie strings of her apron, and ran out to greet her, hugging her tightly.

"Lord have mercy Jolene! What in the world are you doing here? I thought you were coming later in the summer. Why, I don't have dinner ready yet. The roast is ready but I just put the greens on. I know you must be starved." As usual, all the time Mae Belle Brown was fussing, she was reaching in the back seat getting Jolene's purse and bags, setting them down on the ground. Jolene was a wonderful daughter who had been raised to be the best at whatever she tried. She was an avid churchgoer who went with her parents and she'd always been pretty level headed.

"Hello, Mother. I love you too." As the two embraced, Cole Brown strode toward the house in his usual manner until he was sure that the car in front of the cottage was Jolene's. He tried to conceal his shock when he realized Jolene had driven so far and voiced his objection.

"Jolene, for Christ's sake! Tell me girl, that you did not drive that car all the way from New York to West Virginia by yourself? Do you realize how dangerous a thing you've done?"

"But Daddy...."

"Don't you Daddy me! If you weren't as old as you are, I'd put you across my knee and spank you. Now get over here right now and give me a hug before I change my mind and spank you anyway." Jolene knew her Daddy loved her dearly and would never be angry with her for being brave. Growing up, whenever there was spanking that needed to be done, Mae Belle did it. Afterwards, she would disappear for a while. Jolene would cry until mainly her feelings stopped hurting and she would sometimes hear her mother crying too.

"All that matters is I'm here and I'm hungry." Professor Brown shook his head as he reached down picking up her suitcases. They walked up the steps and into the front door. Jolene headed for the kitchen. As soon as she got there and inhaled the smell of her mother's cookies, she instinctively reached into the cabinet to get her favorite glass for an ice old glass of milk to accompany them.

"I'll have dinner ready in about an hour and in the meantime you are welcome to a few sugar cookies. I just took them out of the oven." Jolene had always loved her mother's baking. She remembered helping her stir the batter for cookies and cakes when she was younger. Her mother always made her feel like what she was doing was so important.

"Stir it just a little more." She'd say.

"Now that's good." She could still hear her mother coaxing her along. She also remembered trying to make sure that after her mother poured most of the batter from the bowl, she got to scrape the last of it into the cake pan. That way she could leave as much as she could in the bowl and on the spoon eating it while her mother put the pans in the oven. Her mother acted as if she didn't noticed.

"What else is for dinner?" Jolene was getting hungrier by the minute. Her mother knew that she was not crazy about beef roast but she would not complain.

"I had planned to have vegetables from the garden with dinner tonight. Your father and I planted a few potatoes, tomatoes, and onions out back and I bought some fresh corn and okra. There's some left-over turkey and dressing in the icebox that I'll warm up for you so everybody can be happy."

"Sound great! I think I'll go and take a quick bath. It won't take long and I'll come back down to help you." Jolene ran out the kitchen but not before giving her mom another kiss on the cheek and grabbing one more cookie.

"Hey you, put that cookie back!" Jolene ran upstairs with her stolen cookie as her mother swatted at her with the dish towel. Jolene was very glad to be home. She cut the hot water on in the bathtub so it could start getting hot. She easily stepped out of her blue jeans and purple and gold NYU t-shirt. She looked at herself in the full length mirror behind the door and thought she wasn't too bad looking though she doubted she'd win a beauty contest. She tied her hair back, removed the rest of her clothes and checked to see if the water was warm enough. After filling the tub half full she stepped in, sat down, and let the water relax her from the long drive home.

Cole Brown didn't hear his wife call him for the second time although it wasn't because he was ignoring her. He had been in deep concentration all day. One of the students he advised had spoken to him about a situation that she was having with one of the other professors. She was a young lady who had not done particularly well in her history class. According to the student, she and one of her classmates studied together, ate together, partied together and even skipped classes a couple of times together. They both made the same bad grades and both girls had expected to have to repeat the course. When the grades were posted at the end of the semester, her classmate received a B and she had failed the course. Professor Brown, not wanting to take sides in the issue, told the student as her advisor, he would need to look into the situation and he would advise her of any recourse. He pondered over the impact the allegation could have on the college. This would not be an easy subject to approach even if it was from one colleague to another and the implications would be even riskier.

"Why, I believe this is the third time I've called your name. Are you all right?" Mae Belle was standing right in front her husband in the living room just off the kitchen but he seemed to be a million miles away. Not wanting to offend her, he quickly stood up, acknowledging her presence in the room.

"I'm sorry honey, what did you say?" He hugged her tightly, bent down and planted a big kiss on her jaw. She was an excellent wife and mother to their daughter and he went out of his way to make sure she knew he appreciated it.

"Is there anything I can do to help you in the kitchen?"

"You can tell me what's on your mind. I haven't lived with you for the past twenty three years without knowing when something was wrong with you. So spit it out." He hugged her again as the two of them walked into the kitchen together.

"It's just a problem that one of the students I've been advising is having. It seems that she feels she has been treated unfairly and has asked me to look into it. If her information is true, it could damage the reputation of one of the young professors." Mrs. Brown could tell from the sound of her husband's voice that whatever the situation was, he was really concerned about it. As she got ready to ask him more questions, Jolene bounced down the stairs and appeared in the kitchen in a crisp white cotton blouse and pastel green knee length skirt.

All during dinner, Cole Brown kept the table talk lively yet his earlier thoughts still bothered him. He concealed his feelings from Jolene by keeping a glib conversation about Valery and how helpful she had been to them during the summer. Jolene could tell her mother had taken a real liking to her too. Her father thought she was really smart withstanding the grief of having lost both her parents just after finishing high school. He saw nothing to prevent her from getting a full work scholarship and keeping her grades in tact at the same time. She was well on her way proving her worth during the summer by following the directions of the secretaries in the administration office, making herself nearly indispensable. Even after Valery had left for New York after the summer was over, secretaries still asked about her.

Dinner was delicious and Jolene helped her mother clear the dishes from the table. After Cole Brown had gone outside to get a breath of fresh air, Jolene and Mrs. Brown made plans for the next day.

"Tomorrow we'll go into town and find you a few things that you can take back to New York with you, providing you don't tell your father. She knew how Jolene loved to shop and would keep it a secret. Jolene held her finger to her lips and then kissed her mother on the cheek.

5

New York or "The Big Apple" was popularized in 1920 by John J. Fitz Gerald, a sports writer for the New York Morning Telegraph. He reportedly had heard the phrase "The Big Apple" used to describe New York's racetracks by two African American stable hands at the New Orleans Fair Grounds. He liked the named and used it in his articles. Soon the name "The Big Apple" as a reference to the City of New York was used by everyone.

Mary found Valery in the linen department when she returned downstairs from signing out. She was looking intently at bed sheets.

"What are you doing?"

"Just looking at these prices and imagining which linens I would buy if I was really shopping."

"Believe me, I know what you mean." Mary had spent more time than she would like to admit, pretending she was a well-known designer from New York, flying frequently to Europe to purchase bolts of material she would use to create fashions for her wealthy patrons. She would be able to buy merchandise with no thought as to how much she had spent. When she finished, she would fly back to New York and have her packages and merchandise shipped back to her storage freight. In reality, she doubted she would ever be so lucky. At any rate, her real interest was in becoming a lawyer. Her work in retail she hoped would be temporal until she could get Valery through college.

"I thought we'd take the ferry and go over to Coney Island. It's been a while since we've been over there. We could also visit the Statue of Liberty."

Valery liked the idea. It had been almost two months since she had tasted a New York frankfurter.

"Let's go."

The street vendor lines were long since this was the height of tourist season. Sticking to her strict budget, Mary took enough money to purchase lunches and snacks, catch the subways, and the ferry rides for the two of them. The buildings, streets, and sights in New York brought an aura of excitement like no other. Children squealed with joy and adults stood in line to order franks with their choice of condiments. Hot dog stands were always in abundance on the street corners. Vendors with never smiling faces were always trying to satisfy customers passing for a quick snack. They had to endure the endless 'frankfurter' orders by parents allowing their children to point to pictures of what they thought they wanted as well as trying to decipher the many languages spoken from tourist all over the world. Mary and Valery stood in line patiently and when it was their time to order, they garnished their franks with mustard, onions, ketchup, and kosher relish.

"We'd better hurry if we're going to make the subway to Manhattan." Mary looked at her watch and then at the bit of hot dog left in sister's hand.

"I might have to get another one before we leave Coney Island coming home". Valery stuffed the last bite in her mouth. After throwing their trash away the two headed for the subway.

The New York City subway, bus routes, and cabs were obvious solutions to getting around without having to worry about so much congestion in and around outlying areas of New York. There were daily runs from Coney Island to Manhattan and back. This would give them a little time to reminisce about some of the fun trips they had taken with their parents. The subway was not as crowded as usual so they found their choice of seating. Once they reached Manhattan, they exited the subway to wait for the next ferry to take them to Coney Island. Once there, they made their way to the ticket booth and purchased a slate of tickets. They rode the bumper cars, the spinning wheel, the merry-go-round, and the Wonder Wheel. They both screamed with delight as the speed and motion of the rides made them dizzy exhilarating the fun. They watched the sideshows of Tom Thumb and his brother as well as the endless attractions that made Coney Island a beloved amusement park.

After spending much of the money Mary had, they decided to walk a bit and take in the Atlantic Ocean breeze. They walked past several booths of culinary delights from many different cultures. The robust flavor of spaghetti and beer or a bottle of wine could be purchased at "The Italian Kitchen" for twenty cents. Twenty cents could also buy you a frankfurter, corn on the cob with butter and salt, and a frozen custard. Venders made good revenue with hundreds of thousands of tourists as well as New Yorkers visiting the islands. The day ended when the two found themselves walking along the Riegelmann Boardwalk, a strip of land that stretched 2.7 miles along the southern shore of the Coney Island Peninsula. They found a spot on the sand, pulled out their beach towels and sat for a while.

"So, tell me all about Blue Keyes State College." Mary really wanted to know if Valery was happy. Mary knew that she could detect if the Browns and her baby sister were really a harmonious match and if West Virginia was where Valery really wanted to study.

"I love West Virginia and the Browns are great! They have been very kind to me and I feel right at home. I haven't had the chance to meet many students other than in passing but I'm sure that will come later.

The two sisters talked in length about their next steps. Mary, about her plans to continue working until Valery finished college and then returning to NYU herself. Valery hopeful that her time at the college would be successful and after her graduation she would find work and in turn help Mary finish law school at NYU.

Mary looked down at her watch and realized that they needed to finish their conversation and head for the pier that would ferry them to Liberty Island. The Statue of Liberty located in New York Harbor was a prodigious, neoclassical sculpture given from the people of France to commemorate the alliance of France and the United States during the American Revolution. It was built as a monumental sculpture that symbolized freedom and justice throughout the world. As children, their parents had taken them there, but it had been a while. Once the ferry embarked at the pier, they exited to what appeared as an even more colossal sculpture.

The statue, which stood over one hundred fifty feet high, looked magnificent with its layers of copper and iron frame. Valery had always thought the name Liberty was quite appropriate as she extended her right hand holding a burning torch representing freedom. The left hand, holding a tablet had the date inscribed on it that the United States was declared its independence. Its importance to the world marked the greeting of thousands of immigrants and visitors as they entered New York Bay and arrived in the United States.

"Wow!" Valery exclaimed. "Isn't she even more beautiful than the last time we saw it?"

"Yes." Mary wished that she had a camera to record these moments of the two of them together. This day regardless would be etched in her mind forever. Visiting the Statue of Liberty was a real treat for any visitor. They had to decide whether they would ride the elevator or climb the first 192 steps to the observation area at the top of the statue's pedestal. Mary and Valery decided to be adventuresome and walk the stairs. Once there, they took a short break and continued another 162 steps toward her crown. The steps became narrower with only one rail on the right side and a large column that helped hold the massive statue's form. From the crown, they could see a portion of her right arm looming in mass and the very bottom of the touch in all of its grandeur. After taking it all in, they walked back down the stairs to the base of the statue.

"What an experience!" Valery exclaimed. There was very little else that could excite the senses like the sights of New York City.

"Hey, let's go." Mary could see they had little time before the ferryboat would be leaving for the harbor exchange to Manhattan. The ferry boat ride was fun and they enjoyed looking at the statue of liberty fade further away. They exited the ferry boat and made their way to the 86th Street subway entrance. Mary purchased two tokens at the window and the two of them went through the turnstile where they would wait for the next train to come. A couple stood closely together arm in arm, looking as if they were truly in love while another man wearing a red beret and army fatigues stood vigilantly. There were businessmen dressed in dark suits and ties with briefcases, and an elderly Jewish woman dressed in traditional attire bending wearily over her cane.

As the subway train approached, passengers could hear the click-clack of its wheels nearing the platform track. Passengers began moving closer as the train came to a halt. When the doors opened, the passengers rushed to get on, as was custom to try and get a seat. Once everyone had boarded, the doors closed and the train cars began to move slowly on the rails at first and then faster and faster. All passengers were encouraged to hold onto the train's handrails if they were not seated, to avoid losing their balance while riding. Mary and Valery were standing up near the front part of the train and were holding onto the hand railing. They would be riding through a few stops before they reached their Manhattan destination. There were stops at Bedford Park Boulevard, 96th Street, 103rd Street, and at 110th Street. As passengers got off the subway, it left more and more empty seats. Although the seats were for any passenger, in 1941, Mary and Valery both knew that it was always better to wait. If anyone else was headed for the seat they would continue to stand. After everyone settled down for the ride to the next stop, there was one seat left. A white gentleman in every sense of the word immediately got up and gestured to Mary to take his seat. She appreciated his kindness and sat down. Valery too, had spotted an empty seat and all the people within visual range expected her to sit in it. Valery walked toward the seat. She smiled at the Jewish woman recognizing her as the same person that was waiting at the subway platform earlier. She turned and began to sit down. The old lady began shouting at her.

"No! Don't sit beside me nigger, nigger, nigger, nigger, nigger, nigger, nigger." Her voice was high and shrill as she called Valery a nigger the first time and each time thereafter the pitch was lower and lower until the last one came out and she buried her head on her cane. She closed her eyes and didn't open them again. Several men immediately jumped from their seats and offered their seat to Valery. She was now frightened and had not expected such a blatant response from the woman. Valery sprang up and clung to the railing looking down at the subway floor willing the tears not to surface until she could at least get off the subway. Mary immediately stood up and joined her sister at the rail. She turned so the passengers closest to Valery could not see her face. Mary was as angry as Valery was embarrassed and felt that she say something in defense of her sister. But before she had a chance to say anything, both of the white men that were sitting on either side of the old woman stood up with Valery and refused to sit beside her. One man came over to the girls trying to keep his balance amidst the rocking of the rail car.

"She is just an old, bitter woman." Another man said, "Don't pay her any attention." And still another one shook his head at the old lady as he exited the train and said, "Foolish woman." The subway by then was coming to the stop at 116th Street. As Mary and Valery exited subway, they didn't say anything for a while. Mary wanted to give her younger sister a chance to decide if she wanted to mention the incident on the subway or talk about something else. They made one last stop to buy homemade ice cream cones from the nearby creamery before they walked the last few blocks to their apartment. For some reason the ice cream had a way of soothing the trouble she had faced. Once they reached the apartment, Valery did talk about what had happened earlier on the subway.

"Do you think if my skin was lighter like yours, she would have treated me that way?"

"I don't know. She was an awful person. She didn't even know you, because if she had, she would have known that you are a great person and my fabulous sister!" Mary pointed to the ceiling and as Valery looked up, Mary took a bite of Valery's ice cream cone. When Valery realized her sister had tricked her, they both let out a burst of laughter that made them forget about the whole incident. At least Mary thought she did. With the rest of the time Valery had before returning to Blue Keyes State College, the two cooked together, went window shopping after Mary came home from work, and went to Harlem's Apollo Theater to see African American performers like Bessie Smith, Billie Holliday, Dinah Washington, and Count Basie.

Jolene had come back to spend a few days with Mary and Valery before she too had to return to NYU. On the last night the three would be together for a while, they decided to pull an all-night slumber party. Jolene had brought her phonograph and vinyl recordings of their favorite jazz artists. Hair flailing in the air, feet moving and skirts raised to the popular dances like the Charleston, the scissors, and the mess around. They popped corn in their black cast iron skillet, baked cupcakes, and made cold cut sandwiches and danced, laughed, and talked until dawn.

Having gotten little sleep, Valery woke up at 8:30 that morning and tried to quickly pack and make it to the bus station. By the time Mary, Jolene, and she reached the bus terminal, it had left, leaving Valery without transportation to get back to West Virginia. Jolene came up with an idea. If Valery gave the money she would have paid for her bus ticket to Jolene for gas, Jolene could drive Valery back to the campus. Mary wanted to go with them but she couldn't afford the time off from work. It was agreed upon but this time Jolene did call her parents and let them know.

"Are you sure you want to do this, Jolene?" Mrs. Brown would never tell Jolene she couldn't come home even though she had just left West Virginia days earlier. She thought about it and decided that she would explain to her husband that this was an extenuating circumstance and that

Jolene really couldn't say no to Valery. She'd still have a few days to get back to New York before it was time to begin classes at NYU.

"Yes, Mother. Mary and Valery are my good friends and I want to help. Tell Daddy I'll be very careful. Don't forget me in your prayers. I love you Mother. See you soon." Since the drive would take nearly fourteen hours, Jolene decided to go back to the apartment and get a little more sleep before taking on the trip to West Virginia. At four o'clock that afternoon, she and Valery left New York headed for Blue Keyes State College.

6

Valery could tell they were nearing West Virginia as she looked into the early morning fog. Beyond the mist, the blue-ridged mountains in all their majesty stood boldly as if beckoning her to her new home. As they snaked through the narrow two-lane roads she could almost see Mrs. Brown's smile and smell the aromas from the kitchen. She felt no disappointment. The campus was quiet as they made their way to the cottage home. Valery already missed Mary but felt at home as she got of the car to stretch her legs. She'd get her suitcases later. As they entered the house, the smell of hickory smoked bacon and homemade biscuits filled their nostrils. Although Valery was hungry, the sight of Mrs. Brown made her happy and she hugged her tightly.

"My dear Valery, I am so glad to see you. How did you enjoy being back home with your sister?" Mrs. Brown stood back and gave Valery the once over showing approval as Valery freely shared the adventures she'd had with Mary while in New York.

"Mary took me to her job at Macy's and I met her boss. We took in Coney Island and Liberty Island. It was great." While she talked, Valery washed her hands in the kitchen sink and wiped them on the towel Mrs. Brown handed her. She thought about the incident on the train with the Jewish woman but decided to not mention it, changing the subject. "I take it Dr. Brown is at the university." Valery was anxious to see him too.

"Yes. He went early this morning. He said something about meeting with some students who needed help to transfer to other classes. Anyway, he knows that you and Jolene are here and he's planning to meet us as soon as his meeting and classes are over."

"Are we going to wait until Daddy gets here before we eat?" Jolene had been eyeing the biscuits for a while and her mother knew that it wouldn't be long before she would reach for one and start nibbling.

"Oh no. I already fixed his plate and left it warming on the stove. He can get it when he gets home." Mrs. Brown, Jolene, and Valery all sat around the table for grace before they began the meal. "Father, thank You for getting our loved ones home safely and for the food we are about to receive for the nourishment of our bodies. Forgive us for our sins in Jesus' Name. Amen." It was a rare moment, but Mrs. Brown enjoyed having a chance to not only talk to her daughter and Valery again, but to do so without her husband present. She couldn't remember a time that the conversation had been livelier. It was nonstop vocal production among the three of them until the sound of the door opening interrupted their conversation.

"Hello everybody!" Cole Brown entered the front door of the cottage and turned right to the kitchen. There, the lovely faces of his wife, daughter, and Valery stared intently as he hugged them all and gestured for his wife not to get up to get his food. He had no problem getting his plate from the stove where he knew she had put it.

"Well, well….I hear you missed your bus." Dr. Brown tried to look sternly at Valery, but he knew it wouldn't work because she was a conscientious person who tried to do everything well. It had probably upset her that she missed the bus and had to make alternate plans.

"Yes, sir." Valery looked down at her plate for a moment. She wasn't sure what she needed to say. Dr. Brown saved her the trouble.

"I have some news to share with everyone. As you know. I have been working here for a number of years in the position of professor. Dean Gilbert called me in this morning to inform me that my duties have been expanded to include some counseling and that my salary would increase too!"

"Congratulations!" The chorus of three sang as each rejoiced from a different thought processes. Valery hoped that her relationship with the Brown's would help her get the maximum scholarship funds she so desperately needed during her four year stay at Blue Keyes State. Jolene was happy because it would give her father more status at the college and build his resume. Mae Bell Brown relished the thoughts of having a more money in the household to spend, not to mention the possibility of buying that lovely winter coat she had spied hanging in the window of Bradley's, a well-to-do clothing store on Government Street downtown. Dr. Brown was happy because it would give him a chance to help more students make good choices about their futures.

Advising students had always seemed like one of the most important jobs that one could ascertain. He knew of some situations when a student had not been able to graduate when they had expected because someone had given them ill advice. He had never been that way. Along with preparing the syllabi for his classes, Dr. Brown would always ask his secretary to make him a folder for each student he advised. The information accumulated in the folders gave him an opportunity to study the profile of each student. He would initially set up times to meet with each student, verify and update the information, and offer feasible advice concerning class schedules. He often suggested that a student take a particular class from a faculty member based on the students' personality. Dr. Brown's reputation had preceded him and students sought him to be their advisor. Some teachers envied his popularity with students based on ratio of student to staff. After all, many faculty advisors felt one should not have to "nursemaid" a student through the academic process since each student had a copy of the school's catalog and a handbook.

The Dean of Student Affairs had requested a meeting with Dr. Brown when a few letters of his over-attention to students by a few faculty members reached his office. He was impressed. He knew that if any faculty advisor could affect areas of weaknesses in his department, it was Cole Brown. He waited outside Dean Gilbert's office until his secretary told him to go in. The two men had known each other for a while. They shook hands and Dean Gilbert offered him a seat.

"I see that you are building quite a rapport advising students."

"Thank you sir. I try to make sure that when these students leave Blue Keyes State, they will have had a good experience both academically and socially. I believe that as word of mouth reaches the parents that we spend quality time building their child's confidence both academically and socially, they will sing the praises of this college all over the country. This way, everyone gets the maximum benefit from the institution."

Before Cole Brown knew it, he had spent an hour with Dean Gilbert and had impressed him so much that the dean immediately asked him about moving up in his department. He did not hesitate to tell him he thought professors with tenure, higher ranks, and more years of experience would be very upset if he was awarded a higher status and a salary increase.

"We have a competent and well-trained staff here, as you know. I am sure that most have the interest of students as their priority. I am sure that no staff member would begrudge the opportunity for the school to become one of the top in the country. We work together as a team to make this college the best it can be. Thank you for accepting your new duties and congratulations! Cole Brown knew that no further conversation would be necessary as Dean Gilbert's work was final.

7

Breakfast, as usual, had been wonderful and the Brown family and Valery had a wonderful reunion of sorts. The rest of the day was filled with getting Valery to her assigned dorm, finding the matron to secure the keys to her room, and later looking for some of the staff and student workers she had met during the summer. Mrs. Brown and Jolene stayed with Valery during the better part of the day so she would have a sense of family with her. Valery introduced them as her Godmother and sister. There were lots of girls coming and going on the first day of registration. There were students from practically all fifty states. Long lines plagued the registration tables as students filled out forms and tried to find jobs on campus to help pay their tuitions. Jobs would soon be at a premium since there would be more students that needed them than availability would provide. Valery was glad that with Dr. Brown's help she had secured a job and had already registered. As the day wore on, it seemed that tempers became shorter on both the parts of the students and the college working staff.

"I'm sorry ma'am. I can't read your writing. Where are you from?"

"I'm from Freehole, New Jersey."

"From where? I can't hear you. Could you please speak up?" Edith, the student in line had never been so embarrassed in her life. She had deliberately said the name of the town almost inaudibly hoping that no one except the person on the other side of the table would hear her. It seemed though as if the student worker was determined to make her say it loudly enough to make fun of it.

"I see. And could you spell that for me, please?" Edith knew for sure that he was mocking her now but she knew that she had no choice but to comply with his wishes, since she could not go any further without being a registered student.

"F-r-e-e-h-o-l-e."

"Well, thank you. Now just to be sure, please pronounce that one more time." Edith knew that this idiot would not stop taunting her until she said it more loudly and by now she too had lost her patience.

"Freehole!" Edith shouted so loudly that several other registration workers looked up from their posts. To humiliate her further, the student worker then passed her paperwork on to the next student worker. "Watch out everybody. This is Edith Halloway from Freehole, New Jersey." All of the freshman students within earshot of the comment began snickering at first, and then more with other students straining to hear and asking others why everyone was laughing. Edith tried to laugh too, but as her eyes brimmed with tears, she wondered if she should have come to West Virginia or gone to a college in New Jersey. Her father owned a small merchandise store there and he was very proud to be financially able to send his daughter away to college. Edith knew too, truth being told, that her father had been very eager to get her out of the town. He thought she had begun to take a serious look at Curtis, one of the locals, of which he did not approve.

"Better get her out of here while she's willing to go." She had overheard her father telling one of his friends one night after he thought she'd gone to bed. What her father didn't know was that Curtis was not special to her. They attended the same high school but his interest was in her best friend Pauline. Pauline wanted nothing to do with him but Curtis begged Edith to intercede on his behalf. Edith felt sorry for him and approached the subject to Pauline.

"I don't have any time for that silly buck-toothed boy." Pauline was not only spoiled but could be very condescending at times. Still Edith tried to help.

"Come on Pauline. He's really a nice person. I'm sure you would like him if you gave him a chance.

"If he's so nice, why don't you be his girlfriend? Your daddy would be thrilled." Pauline knew that Edith's daddy was overprotective. Nobody was ever good enough for his baby girl. When she was old enough to go to the movies with a young suitor, she would make sure that her boyfriend knew that her daddy would be accompanying them. It didn't take long before word got out that Edith's daddy was as mean as a rattle snake when it came down to hanging around her. She hardly had time to talk to boys anyway since she went to school during the day, did her homework and chores around the house after school, and then on most days walked to her daddy's store about a half mile down the road to help out and then she and her father would ride home.

It was always a lot of fun watching people come and go at the store. It was one day that Curtis was particularly aggravated with Pauline for letting another boy kiss her after school that he threw all caution to the wind and came boldly in to see Edith at her daddy's store.

"That girl done gon' crazy! Do you know what she did today?"

"No, Curtis. But I have a feeling you're going to tell me."

"She kissed him. I saw it with my own eyes. She actually kissed him."

"She kissed who? Edith tried to sound concerned even though she knew that if he had only seen Pauline kiss a boy once, he was lucky. Pauline planted kisses on lots of boys.

"That Ralph Philpott. He's been after her for the past few months trying to get her attention and all. I'm gonna have a little talk with him after school tomorrow and if he doesn't have a good explanation, I'm going to knock his…"

"Now hold on there. C'mon. Let's walk outside for a little while. You need to really clear your head. Edith had wanted to tell Curtis for the longest time that Pauline wasn't interested in him but she didn't want to hurt him. She thought he would get tired of trying to attract her attention and find another girl to think about. But he didn't so Edith felt it was time to do the only thing she knew to do. At first, she shuttered to think what he would say or do because she knew he had a bad temper. She thought he might even be angry at her for not telling him sooner.

Much to her surprise, Curtis took it much better than she had thought. For the next few days, she tried to talk to him as much as possible, until it became apparent that he no longer seemed to care about Pauline so much. They continued to talk a lot and soon it became obvious that Curtis' attention had shifted from Pauline to her. Somewhere in the midst of it all, her very observant father decided that this boy had gotten too close to his daughter and it was then that he began talking about her going to a school away from home after her high school graduation. It really didn't matter too much to Edith. Freehole was a small town in New Jersey and it would be a welcomed relief to go to a place where there was an opportunity to get a good education and meet more people. However, Edith was not quite prepared for the welcome party she had just received in the registration line from a boy that she thought she could whip if it ever came down to it. She hoped that one day she might get the chance to do it.

8

Valery finished putting the finishing touches on her dorm room. She had planned to meet with the Brown's later on for an early dinner. Jolene was planning to leave the next day and she wanted to make sure that she spent some time with her before her departure. She also was planning to spend her first official night on the campus. Mrs. Brown had given Valery a beautiful peach-colored bedspread and matching curtains that she had made for her. Valery had brought the few pictures she had of her family and had hung them thoughtfully on the wall. A picture of her mother and father a year before the accident that claimed their lives, and a current picture of her sister Mary. She wanted to put a picture of the Brown family on the wall too, but thought better of it when she realized the possibility of students thinking her relationship with the family would give her a leg up or that she would be labeled a campus snitch. She would never compromise her relationship with Professor Brown and so she resisted the temptation. Valery's thoughts were distracted by a gentle knock on the door.

"Come in."

"Hello. I'm Charlene Welch and if you're Valery Lewis, then I'm your new roommate."

"Hi. I'm Valery. Glad to meet you. I took the top bunk but if you would prefer it, I don't mind switching with you."

"Oh, no. I wouldn't dream of it. I'll be very comfortable right here. Thanks."

"I was just going out for a bit, but I'll be back later and can give you a tour of the campus if you'd like.

"Sounds great. I'm looking forward to it. We can get to know each other a little better then." Charlene was pleased with the introduction she had received from her new roommate.

"See you later." As Valery strolled across the campus, she felt at home. She knew a few instructors by name since she had worked on the campus during the summer. She recognized familiar faces that caught her eye as she made her way to the residential area of the campus. Apartments for single professors as well as small cottages for married couples lined the north end of the campus. Jolene and Mrs. Brown were sitting at the kitchen table drinking a cold glass of lemonade when she arrived.

"Hello there, Miss Freshman. How goes it?" Valery already felt the glow of accomplishment as she poured herself a glass of lemonade from the iced-cold pitcher.

"It's really exciting. You wouldn't believe what I saw on my way over here." It seemed as if there were always stories to tell whenever Jolene, Mrs. Brown and she got together. Cole Brown had been in the family room reading but entered the kitchen just as the three females let a walloping round of laughter.

"Let me guess. You were walking down the campus and saw the cutest boy ever in life." He knew that Valery did not spend time talking or thinking about boys. One of the things that he really admired about her was her no nonsense perspective on life. She was the kind of young lady that would make some young man very proud of her. She seemed to face life courageously, taking to heart every matter and weighing the options before making a decision. He was proud to step in as a sort of surrogate father in the absence of her parents.

"No sir. It was just...oh, never mind." Valery was not going to tell Dr. Brown she had overheard that humiliating situation near the gym over one of the student workers and some girl named Edith from Freehole, New Jersey.

The grace was given and dinner was delicious. Mrs. Brown's kitchen counter was lined with fried fish, baked Cornish stuffed hens, green beans, cabbage and fired okra, sweet potatoes, corn on the cob, cornbread and rolls, peach cobbler and chocolate cake sending sweet aromas in the air and well beyond the screened front door of the small cottage where the Brown's lived. Cole Brown looked fondly at his family as they ate but Mae Belle could tell he was thinking about something other than dinner.

"Penny for your thoughts." Mae Belle had been eyeing her husband.

"Don't bet on it. You might get shortchanged. Actually, I have an organizational meeting later this evening and I must get my reports together so I will have to say my good-byes to my sweet daughter now." He leaned over and kissed Jolene on the cheek reminding her to drive carefully.

"Take care of yourself and don't take any wooden nickels." Jolene teased her father.

Valery decided that she would help Mrs. Brown with the dishes before heading back to the dorm. She remembered she promised to show her new roommate around campus. It didn't take long as the three of them quickly cleared the table and tidied up the kitchen.

"Don't be a stranger around here, Valery."

"Thanks Mrs. Brown. You are the best cook and Godmother any girl could ever dream of having, however, I'd better watch myself. I don't know how many overweight physical education majors Blue Keyes State has had in the past, but I'm sure they'll make me work doubly hard to get this little bulge off that's beginning to show around my midriff." Jolene laughed as she listened to Valery talk. She was so glad she had taken a chance and asked her father to intercede for her to attend college at Blue Keyes. Valery was seemingly a bright student and was sure to do well. She hoped too, that someday she could help Mary get back to NYU and finish the degree in law she wanted.

9

Charlene Welch was sitting on the bed reading when Valery used her key and unlocked the door to their room. She looked up for a moment, smiled and then went back to reading.

"Hi, Charlene. Did you make it to the dining hall for dinner?"

"Yes, but I'm afraid there seemed to be a problem with the seating. I mean, there was room but only certain students were invited to sit at the tables." That seemed like a rather odd statement to make but during the summer Valery never ate in the dining hall since she was not officially enrolled as a student.

"What do you mean?"

"Well, there were several long lines of people standing outside the cafeteria when I got there, but I went in once the door was unlocked. The dining hall was only half full when I got there. There were plenty of tables with empty chairs. When I got ready to sit down at the first available table, this girl looked at me and said the table was taken. I apologized at first but after it happened again and again regardless of where I tried to sit, I lost my appetite and came back here to read. I was hoping you hadn't forgotten that you said you'd walk with me around the campus." Valery didn't want to make a big deal out of what Charlene had just said, and she really didn't want to believe that the students could be that snobbish.

"Don't worry Charlene, they probably are the upperclassmen. We're freshmen, so we'll just stick together." Charlene began to look relieved and even though she was hungry she would tough it out until breakfast.

The next morning, Valery and Charlene left their dorm and began walking down the campus toward the dining hall. They both noticed girls with extremely fair skin and long hair talking to each other. Girls with light brown skin were in one group, while the girls with darker skin were conversing together. Once inside the dining hall, the two girls found an empty table. Other lost looking students came over and asked if they could join them. Soon there were eight people sitting there. After the grace was sung, student waiters, dressed immaculately in white jackets served breakfast. Neither Valery nor Charlene had ever been served in such a manner before and somehow they felt out of place. There was a complete table setting with forks, spoons, knives and a cloth napkin in front of each chair. The breakfast was great and afterwards, she and Charlene walked along the campus looking at all the new faces there were to see. Charlene wondered if she would ever learn her way around Blue Keyes State.

Valery assured her that once she got used to the campus, it would not seem as large. The campus was filled with students from everywhere and many were still in lines trying to pay their fees, some were in the work study lines filling out applications, and some were still trying to get situated into their dorm rooms. They walked the entire campus, familiarizing themselves with the buildings and dorms. It was nearly lunch time and Valery thought since there was a little time to spare, she could at least introduce Charlene to the staff members she knew in the administration building. Once inside, they walked down the main corridor and rounded the corner just in time to see Dr. Brown.

"Hello Dr. Brown,"

"Valery. I see that you have already met a friend."

"Yes. Friend and roommate. Charlene Wilson, this is Professor Brown. Professor Brown, this is Charlene Wilson. Charlene is from Jackson, Mississippi and will be majoring in English." Dr. Brown extended his hand to Charlene and she likewise did the same.

"Pleased to meet you, Dr. Brown." He was surprised that Charlene had come to Blue Keyes State instead of going to one of the well-known colleges in Mississippi. Charlene wondered if she should tell him she and her parents had met the college president, Dr. Samuel Lee, when he attended an oratorical contest that she entered and won. Dr. Lee was particularly impressed with Charlene's delivery of the speech and offered her a scholarship to attend Blue Keyes State College. However, just as she got ready to respond, Dr. Brown suggested that if the girls hadn't made prior plans for lunch, they could have lunch with him and Mrs. Brown. Valery was thrilled that Dr. Brown had extended the invitation since she wanted to but didn't know whether it would be an appropriate thing to do.

Mrs. Brown waved from the front door when she saw Valery. She was glad Valery had found a friend.

"Oh, do come in." Mrs. Brown echoed when she saw Valery through the screen door.

"Hello, Mrs. Brown. Dr. Brown told us to come over. He said he knew you would not mind but if this isn't a good time…"

"Of course it's a good time. It's always a good time when I get a chance to see you." Mrs. Brown had come to know Valery well as she planted a kiss on her cheek.

"And who is this lovely young lady?"

"This is my roommate Charlene Wilson from Jackson, Mississippi."

"I'm so glad to have you in our home. Come on in and sit down. I was just getting ready to set the table for lunch."

"May I help?" Valery was so happy that she had run into Dr. Brown. At least Charlene would get a chance to meet some very nice people.

"Sure." Mrs. Brown had prepared potato salad, baked beans, deviled eggs and barbecued chicken. Charlene couldn't believe that this was considered lunch since her lunch normally consisted of a cold cut sandwich with lettuce, tomato, and mayonnaise, a piece of fruit and occasionally a slice of cake with milk. Jackson was a town where communities stuck together. Charlene lived there with her parents and brothers. There usually wasn't a lot of time to eat since there was so much work to do on the farm. Her mother would pack sandwiches and lots of lemonade for the boys and her so they could eat quickly and get back to work whenever they weren't in school.

Dr. Brown was glad he had run into the girls. He had not had a chance to prepare Valery for what her first day as a freshman might be like.

"Now about this evening, I think you should know there might be some things said and done during the vesper hour that my startle you somewhat, but believe me, it's all a part of being a freshman."

10

At 6:15 that evening, the bell for vespers rang. According to the student handbook, vespers was every Wednesday and Sunday evening at 6:30. Everyone had to be in his or her seat prior to that time. At exactly 6:30, President Samuel Lee, flanked by his brigade of distinguished faculty members ceremoniously walked onto the stage and all of the students rose. The ROTC brought in flags, pledges were recited, and the national anthem was sung. It had been a long tradition of the school to begin the vesper hour of a new school year the same way. This year had been no exception. President Lee was a tall, statuesque man. As he rose and strolled to the podium on the stage, he reminded Valery of the way George Washington Carver must have looked as the world finally acknowledged his many contributions to the science world. President Lee only had to open his mouth once to let you know by his eloquent mannerisms and superb speaking ability that he was in charge of Blue Keyes State College and if you didn't adhere to his authority, your stay there would be brief. He began to deliver his speech by addressing the class of 1941-1942.

"Let me begin by saying, you have reached a pinnacle in your life. It is by no small chance that you have been given an opportunity that many request but all are not granted. Our country is in the midst of a crisis with soldiers being carried off to war every day. Thank your God above each night for the opportunity that He has given you. I trust that each of you have read his or her handbook. You are expected to do so and I will not hesitate to ask you henceforth from this day forward any question that is

55

answerable from that little jewel. This means that you will only be allowed to attend your classes, eat in the dining hall and go to the library. Reading, ladies and gentlemen is a fundamental tool in our society and you will read. There have been too many people that have given their very lives for you to have the right to read. Read everything and every chance you get. Read to be enlightened of the world and its social status. Read because your forefathers were bludgeoned for having the desire to do so. There will come a day when your ability to read may save your life. There will be no misconduct between males and females on this campus. If you are involved in misconduct, you will be given a one way ticket to the place from whence you came. You will not only bring shame to your family but you will never be allowed admittance to any other state funded college. Refer to your handbook and discover any other particulars concerning dorm rules. We have very fine matrons and proctors who will be monitoring your activities day in and day out. These ladies and gentlemen are highly trained in the area of male and female antics and will not hesitate to turn your name in whereby, you, as a deterrent of this fine college, will be expelled. Many of your parents have sacrificed a great deal for you to be here. If you are a work study student, make sure that you are always on time for your job. It will be no different once you graduate and leave this institution. You must show responsibility. Wear clothing that exemplifies you as a person who respects others and can be an asset in whatever walk of life you choose to pursue. Let today be the beginning of the rest of your life. In closing, I would like to get to know each and every one of you by name. As I see you walking about on the campus, I will often stop to talk to you. Make sure you keep yourself abreast of the world around you as not to appear as the uninformed citizen that many others would like to assume you are. Have a good year. God bless you."

After President Lee finished his oration, the student body was led in applause by the faculty on stage. A few brief remarks were made before the upperclassmen were dismissed to go to their perspective dorm areas.

Steven Cook, the student government president was then asked to come forward and speak to the freshmen. Valery recognized Steven Cook as the student worker that was rumored to have humiliated the freshman from Freehole, New Jersey.

Valery and Charlene waited, like all the other freshmen for more instructions. Steven made his way to the microphone and after brief remarks, asked all freshmen to leave the chapel and go to the gymnasium. The students were obedient and left the chapel walking quietly to the gym. The females were told to move to the front left and all the males, were instructed to move to the front right. Once there, Steven motioned for all students to be seated and took the microphone.

"Again, I'm Steven Cook your student government president and delighted that you are here. Being that you are in your first year at Blue Keyes State College, we always try our best to make you feel welcome. Each of you now entering as freshmen will take on a new name. As of this moment, and for the next six weeks, you will be enrolled in a probationary program designed to acquaint you with real college life. Each of you will be given a 'dog tag' to wear around your neck at all times. You will also receive a beanie that will adorn your head at all times." He looked menacingly at the students and then continued.

"Failure to wear your proper paraphernalia will result in non-admittance to any social functions on and off campus. Your 'dog tag' will have your name and where you are from on it. It will also let other upperclassmen know who their "homies" are. It too is a tradition that all freshmen are called "dog' or 'doggette' depending on your gender. You must wear your tags and beanies when you are awake and when you are asleep. Your beanie is part of your protection and without it, you may be subjected to longer probational periods. There will be no make-up worn by any freshman during this time. If a freshman is caught wearing make-up, all freshmen will be punished. Punishment for freshmen will be determined by a council of your peers. As you hear your name called, you are to walk expeditiously toward the front, pick up your paraphernalia and quietly leave the gym.

"Are there any questions?" There was a hush over the audience as the freshmen looked at each other in disbelief. Even the girls who had earlier looked so pretentious were shocked that they would not be allowed to wear make-up. When Valery's name was called, she dutifully got to the front, picked up her things, and exited the building. She waited for Charlene right outside the door and the two walked quietly back toward the dorm. They were met with jeers and laughter from the upperclassmen waiting to taunt them knowing they could do nothing about it. Once the beanies were given to each freshman, they had to put them on regardless of how long it had taken them to style their hair for their first day on campus. The beanies looked ridiculous. She hoped that Professor Brown could help her if at all possible with the stupid beanie and dog tag rule. Once they reached their dorm, they both sat on the bottom bunk and quietly whispered in hushed tones what they really thought about the meeting they had just attended. After they fussed about the whole idea, they both had to laugh and wonder if it would be funny to them next year when they would become sophomores. Valery didn't think so.

Valery found out that Charlene was one of eight children and was the only one to complete the twelfth grade. All seven of her older brothers had to abandon their dreams of going to college, not because they could not pass the work, but because they had to work on the family's farm harvesting the crops and getting them to market. Charlene worked on the farm too and fully expected to work alongside her brothers. However, she had been an exceptional student in school, not only doing her homework and making high marks, but also always finding a way to make learning fun for herself and her classmates. Even her high school English teacher, Harriet Broomfield took an interest in Charlene after she wrote her first play for her classmates to perform. She wrote well always knowing which of the classmates were best suited for roles. She also wrote beautiful poetry whenever she had time. The teachers at her school were all impressed with her but it was Miss Broomfield who talked Charlene's father Charlie into letting her enter the Southern Baptist Oratorical Contest. The letter had been sent to Bluestone Baptist Church in Jackson. The pastor thought it would be a good opportunity for their best youth speaker. Miss Broomfield had been assigned to the youth and young adult department of the church. Charlene and two other high school seniors had advanced to the final competition stage and the winner would receive a scholarship to the college of their choice. It was there that Charlene's deliverance of her speech won the competition and her scholarship to Blue Keyes State College.

11

Valery was glad Charlene Welch from Jackson, Mississippi was her roommate. She seemed to be a girl who knew what she wanted despite the fact she was a long way from home. Charlene asked Valery all about her hometown in New York since she knew nothing about The Big Apple. She hoped to visit some day, but for now she would settle for understanding the culture through her roommate's experiences. Valery carefully chose her words as she shared her childhood and life growing up in the city. For the first time she was glad that when she spoke of her parents and the accident that claimed their lives, she did so without crying. She told her of the relationship Mary had with Professor Brown's daughter Jolene, which really turned out to be the reason she was attending Blue Keyes State College. She told Charlene her goal was to finish school so her sister, who had to withdraw to help Valery, could return to NYU. They continued to talk about their families until a knock on the door interrupted their conversation. The door, lightly ajar, was opened.

"You must be Valery Lewis and you are Charlene Welch." She was a young woman whose name was Joyce and who would be working the night shift as the dorm matron.

"I will be on duty tonight and just wanted you two to know that if you need anything at all, my door is right across the hall from yours."

"Thank you very much."

"I know that you must feel awkward being away from your homes but it won't take too long to adjust to your new surroundings." Joyce lowered her voice when she spoke the next words to the Valery and Charlene.

"Don't worry about the probation thing. It will be over in no time. And if you ask me, I think it's a silly thing to do anyway. Valery wasn't sure if this was some kind of trick that was being played on them to get them to talk, but she thought it best to just smile and make no comment.

"Your suite mates are the two girls that live in the room right behind you. Their names are Edith and Geraldine. Geraldine just got settled in so it will probably be morning before you'll meet them. The four of you will have to share the bathroom, so don't wait until the last minute to get ready in the mornings. Remember to be on time for breakfast and wear your beanies and dog tags.

"Goodnight ladies." Joyce waved as she closed the door softly behind her. She was glad all the freshmen girls in Frazier Hall were accounted for now she could relax and wait for the ritualistic tap on her window. Oscar, a maintenance worker and she had been lovers for the past few years. She had met him one day after a number of the freshmen girls had complained about several first floor toilets being clogged. She checked and assumed that someone had not been careful to dispose of their sanitary napkins as they had been instructed. She contacted the administration office and was told to call the maintenance department and have them send someone right over. Oscar had worked all day on another full time job and was working part time at Blue Keys State to make a little extra money. He, like many other Negro men, was not financially able to go to college and since he did not meet draft selection requirements, he had found alternate work. It was late that evening before Oscar could get to Frazier Hall. He entered the building and went to the door marked "Matron Only." When Joyce opened the door, their eyes met and she immediately dropped them as it was impolite to stare at a strange man too long. It would be perceived that she was wanton of him and Joyce certainly didn't want to give that impression even though he was quite handsome. He pretended that he didn't see the little glitter in her eye and asked if he could check to see what work was needed to repair the problem in the bathroom.

"Where is the work area ma'am?"

"It's down the hall and to your left. I'll show you."

"I think I can find it. Thanks anyway." Oscar wouldn't have minded her showing him the way but he thought he'd better make sure that she knew his intentions were honorable. Joyce thought she'd better give him some friendly advice before he got himself in a world of trouble.

"Wait. I'd better make sure there are no young ladies in there before you go in. We wouldn't want to start a ruckus now would we? Joyce smiled and looked more intently at him. Oscar didn't respond readily but thought to himself that she was one of the most beautiful women he'd ever laid eyes on.

"I guess not." Joyce opened the door and called to see if anyone was inside but there was no answer.

"It's all yours." She walked casually back down the hall and went into her room. Once inside, she slumped into the nearest chair and wondered how in the world a man that handsome ended up in her dorm. Luck she guessed. It didn't take long for him to solve the problem. Oscar thought he'd let her know for security reasons, he had finish and was leaving. Her door was open and he saw the contour of her body as she stood at her dresser combing her hair.

"All finished ma'am. That should take cares of the problem." Oscar wanted to ask her if he could come back the next day to make sure that everything was all right but he knew that it would end up being an uncomfortable situation for him as it always was when it came down to making acquaintances. Being around people that were educated made him uneasy. He always worried he would say the wrong word and end up being the butt of the jokes at the cafeteria tables among the students and faculty so he said very little.

"Haven't seen you around here much. Just started working here?"

"Been here a few months."

"How do you like your job?"

"Fine. Oscar's short answers made Joyce realize that she had run of questions to ask him but decided she'd try one more time.

"My name's Joyce Smith."

"Oscar Mills. Pleased to meet you. I'd shake your hand but I'm kind of dirty and all, but maybe some other time."

"Yes. That would be nice. Goodnight Oscar." Joyce found lots of faulty maintenance that had to be repaired in Frazier Hall and before too long their continued professional relationship turned into a budding romance. Joyce usually worked the evening shift in the dorm and sometimes the night shift. The girls in Frazier Hall were always glad when she worked since she never really gave them a lot of trouble if they came in a littler after curfew. After she checked all the rooms she usually would not open her door anymore that night. Oscar was usually there, but none of the girls ever said anything about it. And besides that, she was really a nice person.

For some reason, Valery didn't sleep very soundly that night. She had too many things on her mind. She needed to get in touch with Mary since she hadn't spoken to her since the day she left New York for the fall semester at Blue Keyes State. She also wondered what would be in store for her as a freshman. When she did go to sleep, she dreamed of being in her New York brownstone with Mary. She could hear the sounds of applause right outside her bedroom. When she opened the door, myriad's of faces peered and pointed at her. They were all wearing black beanies and their dog tags. Suddenly she realized they were all laughing at her because she wasn't wearing hers! The dream startled her as she awakened realizing it was the next day. There was a stream of light coming from under the door that led to the bathroom. A moment later, Valery heard the sound of running water and assumed her suite mates were taking baths and getting ready for breakfast. Valery laid back on her bed for a few minutes thinking about her silly dream and wondering what would happen if one of the freshmen did forget to wear their paraphernalia. The student handbook indicated that all freshmen were to be at the dining hall at 7:15 that morning. Valery quietly looked in her dresser drawer without turning on the light and felt around trying to decide on what to wear. It was nearly an hour later when Valery still heard running water in the bathroom. She and Charlene now only had fifteen minutes to get to the dining hall.

"Charlene, wake up! We've got to get dressed and get to the dining hall. Charlene was groggy and didn't know what to think."

"Okay, okay. Just give me a minute." When Charlene surfaced to consciousness, and thought about where she was and what Valery had just said she jumped up and frantically began looking for her towel, wash cloth, toothpaste, and toothbrush.

"I need to take my bath."

"We don't have time. Just put on some clothes. We can bathe later."

"Don't forget your beanie and your dog tags." Now Charlene was really aggravated.

"Great. I'm really looking forward to it."

The two barely made it to the dining hall before the door was closed. The cafeteria manager, a tall, swarthy, stout woman was standing at the front of the hall. As she spoke, the hall fell silent.

"Good morning. Thank you for those of you who made it to the dining hall on time. You will begin filling the tables to my left and proceed counterclockwise until everyone is seated. Seating should not take more than fifteen minutes. After which, the upperclassmen will come in and do the same. Once everyone has been seated, we will all stand, grace and then everyone will be served. There will be student waiters bringing your meals. There will be no getting up from our tables unless you are leaving the dining hall. If there are no questions, let's begin." It seemed to Valery that the matter-of-fact sounding cafeteria manager didn't give the students a chance to ask any questions. The two girls filed in one behind the other. It didn't take longer than fifteen minutes before all the freshmen were seated and the upperclassmen began coming in dressed stylishly.

"Good morning Dogette Lewis." Valery looked up to a freckled face boy staring at her as if he knew her.

"Good morning." She responded purely out of politeness.

"My name is Rodney Biggs. I remember seeing you the first day I got on campus. I'm from Columbus, Ohio." They exchanged pleasantries for a moment and each person at the table took the liberty of introducing themselves and sharing a bit of information about their hometown. Once the last upperclassman was seated, everyone stood and the grace was sung. Valery had never been in the cafeteria for breakfast and therefore didn't know the song. Neither had she ever heard the sound of such beautiful voices before in her life. It was as if all the upperclassmen were music majors. Each sound seemed to fill every crevice of the dining hall with beautiful harmony and Valery both felt embarrassed to not be able to contribute to its melodiousness. At the moment it looked as if the freshmen would get away with not singing until President Lee walked in the dining hall and looked in the general direction of the room where little sound was being emitted. Valery remembered that the President at vespers had admonished all students to be aware of all the information included in the handbook and the words to the song were there. She was glad that he didn't ask the freshmen to stand up and sing it. Once everyone was seated, the student waiters, dressed in white long-sleeved shirts, black slacks and black bow ties, came forth with platters of sausage patters, eggs, grits, toast, and fresh fruit.

There were five other females seated around the table with Valery and the two males were seated beside each other. When the waiter placed the sausage on the table, Rodney immediately picked up the platter scraped off several extra sausage patties leaving some with no sausage to eat until the waiters came around a second time. Valery thought that Rodney was selfish not to give everyone a chance to have at least one sausage patty, but she said nothing. He didn't even seem to care just continued to eat and talk as if there was nothing wrong. After all the platters were passed around, Valery had a piece of toast on her plate and some grits. She quickly realized that having a meal in the dining hall would become survival of the fittest.

"Who are your suite mates?" Valery couldn't believe Rodney 'eat-all-the-food' Biggs stopped eating long enough to ask a question. She had to bite her tongue, but managed to respond without a hint of irritation.

"Their names are Edith and Geraldine. We haven't officially met." Valery replied as Charlene, looking disgusted, decided to enter the conversation.

"What dorm are you staying in Rodney?" Charlene felt that it might help if Rodney talked more and gulped his food less.

"Ballard. The dorm for male freshmen. It's the two-story with a basement. The basement is off limits for the freshmen, of course. My cousin Harry is a sophomore and he says he usually doesn't go down there but most of the time it's football players or fraternities, meeting for different reasons.

What time does your first class start?" Rodney didn't want to spend too much time talking. Charlene looked at the Timex watch her father and mother had given her before she left and realized that she needed to go back to the dorm, take a quick bath and get to class on time.

"I have a nine o'clock psychology class in the administrative building and I've got to go back to the dorm before I go."

"My class is there too. I guess I'll see you then." Some of the students had already begun leaving the dining hall before Valery and Rodney left. Once outside, they looked toward the direction of the dorm where a small congregation of upperclassmen, marked only by the nonexistence of their beanies and dog tags, seemed to be surrounding one of the freshman. As they got closer, Valery recognized Edith and a group of boys surrounding her.

"Hey baby, where're you from?"

"Did you say, Freehole, New Jersey?

"Well, if that's true, I'll be over to see you tonight." Laughter erupted among the group.

"Hey! Leave her alone!" The sound of Rodney's voice made the males stop taunting her. They left but not before hurling a few more slurs as they went their way. Valery didn't like what she had heard nor did she think the boys should get away with humiliating Edith like that. Edith looked relieved and wanted to let them know.

"Thanks. It's good to know that there's someone who understands what I'm going through. They'd better be glad my brothers aren't here but I'll be fine." Valery waved goodbye to Rodney and she and Edith walked on to their dorm rooms to finish getting ready for their classes.

Once inside her room, Valery looked at her schedule. She would be taking psychology, English literature, and biology on Mondays, Wednesdays, and Fridays. On Tuesdays, and Thursdays, she would attend philosophy of education and algebra 101. Because of overcrowding, there were no day classes for swimming and frankly she was glad. She had never learned to swim and would be thankful for more attention paid to her by the swimming instructor.

"Hey, it's almost time to go." By now, Charlene had taken a quick bath and was dressed. She stood in the doorway talking to their suite mate Geraldine.

"Valery Lewis, meet our suite mate, Geraldine Harry. Geraldine Harry, Valery Lewis."

"Hello. I'm happy to meet you."

"Same here." And this is my roommate Edith. Valery looked at Charlene and they both responded at the same time.

"We've met." Charlene was curious as to why it had taken so long for them to finish in the bathroom and thought it was a good time to ask.

"We noticed that the water ran for a long time this morning so we thought we'd just wait until after breakfast and then work out a schedule with you." Geraldine looked somewhat sheepish as she admitted it was Edith who had taken so much time in the shared bathroom. She intentionally kept the bathroom occupied in fear of what eventually happened anyway. Valery and Charlene both felt sorry for her and looked forward to the day she would no longer have to endure the cruel gestures from the upperclassmen.

Valery's morning had gone well. She was on time for all of her classes. She listened carefully to her professors as each one discussed their syllabus for the semester. Some of the guidelines and expectations were strict and harsh sounding.

"…half of you will fail this class."

"…some of you may want to withdraw from this class." Valery wondered why the professors seemed so strict. It probably was meant to get students to realize the seriousness of their education. She didn't need to be frightened. She knew what she had to do.

Just before lunch Valery went back to Frazier Hall to finally take her bath and get ready to go the cafeteria. As she unlocked the door and turned the doorknob, her eyes gravitated downward and she saw a small piece of paper which she immediately picked up and read. The paper was an advertisement for the 1941 Homecoming Queen Election. It read:

1941 Blue Keyes State College Homecoming Queen
Vote Janice Holly Jones
"She'll Get the Job Done"

Valery wasn't really interested in who became the homecoming queen but she laid the piece of paper on Charlene's bed so she could read it. The key to the lock turned.

"What are going on?" Valery was shocked to hear Charlene speak in such a manner considering her ability to communicate so well.

"Did you just say what are going on?" Charlene was glad Valery had responded that way.

"It's just the latest slang. It doesn't mean anything really. It's just a silly way to say hi." Charlene could tell that Valery was not in the mood for jokes and decided to change the subject.

"How about lunch?"

"Sure. Let's go."

12

The dining hall was really beginning to fill up by the time Valery and Charlene got to the tables that had been reserved for freshmen. The grace was sung and the student waiters brought lunch to each table. There were hamburgers, hot dogs with chili, French fries, lettuce, tomatoes, corn on the cob, a variety of fruits and vanilla ice cream for desert. As the girls ate, they met other new students.

"Did you all see the flyer that was under everyone's door about the voting for homecoming queen?" The girl that asked the question was quite attractive, thin, medium height, with a pug nose and large, bright eyes. She didn't have a name tag but said her name was Peggy. No one knew whether to answer her or not. She might have been planted by the upperclassmen to find out what the freshmen were thinking, hoping to get them in trouble and extend their probation. Peggy took their silence as consent and continued to talk.

"I've heard that there's been talk about running someone against Janice Holly Jones form homecoming queen. I don't mean just anyone but somebody, you know, dark-skinned, like us. There's a meeting tonight at six thirty behind the gym with some of the football players. If you want to come you may, but if you don't, just pay attention to all the notes that are slipped under you door." One boy at the table spoke up.

"What difference does it make? It's just a title and a chance for some girl to be paraded up and down like a puppet and jump every time the administration says so. The handbook even says it in so many words."

"Well, it should make a lot of difference to you." Peggy was indifferent to what she had heard and was determined to get her point across.

"For the last ten years, if you look at some of the old yearbooks in the library, you'll see that all of the former Blue Keyes State College Homecoming Queens had one thing in common. All of them looked white. Can you imagine? We've been laughed at by every other Negro college campuses from here to yonder. For one thing, it says to all the rest of us that we're good enough to pay our money to attend this school, but we're not good enough to represent it. Another thing about it that should concern you is that the student government association officers seem to think that although students elect them, they can control everything we do. We are not allowed to say anything. How did you feel the first day of school when you were marched over to the gym and separated by gender?" You would have thought we were going to have sex with each other right there or something. Then they made all of the freshmen wear demeaning attire and treat you like a little child who needs punishment if you don't."

By this time, Peggy's oration had attracted not only the freshmen who were sitting at the table, but also all the students sitting at the adjacent tables. It had also gotten considerably quiet in that section of the room for those that wanted to hear the conversation.

"So what do you want us to do?"

"Come to the gym tonight and find out." Peggy stood up and left the table but not before she had successfully planted the seed of curiosity in the minds of every freshman in the dining hall. Valery and Charlene finished their lunches and headed back to their dorms to retrieve their books for their evening classes.

"What do you think about Peggy?" Charlene asked.

"You mean about the student government treating us the way they did?"

"That was interesting wouldn't you say?"

"Well, since you asked, I think she's right but I'm not sure that it's enough for us to stick our noses in it. You know once you're labeled as a trouble maker, it'll follow you around like a lost puppy. Professor Brown would be so disappointed if I got in trouble after all he and his wife have done to help me but at the same time, I don't think it would hurt to just go to the meeting." Valery was curious to know more about the traditions of Blue Keyes State College and what could be done about it.

"We'll go together."

"Great! See you then." Valery, books in tow, was off to her classes.

The afternoon was spent meeting more of her professors. They passed out more guidelines for the semester in which Valery noticed lots of assignments that required research. She enjoyed going to the library. It was a place that offered quiet and solitude and you could work without being bothered by anyone. The librarian, Miss Beal was a very intelligent woman who always knew where to find whatever it was that you needed. She also was so fair-skinned that she was often mistaken for being Caucasian. She often laughed when brazen students asked her if she, in fact was.

It was three forty five when Valery finished her last class. She decided to drop by Professor Brown's office to say hello if he wasn't busy.

"Come in." Professor Brown looked up from his desk even though he really didn't have to since Valery was the only person who knocked in a syncopated five-two knock sequence.

"Hello Valery. How has your day been?"

"Fine. And yours?"

"Oh, there are a million things to do but I'll get caught up eventually. We're still getting a few students enrolled I understand. I hear, as a matter of fact, that enrollment is up this semester and projected to be the largest freshman class the college has had so far. I think there are about three hundred total."

"How many upperclassmen are there?"

"Approximately three hundred fifty. You should be proud to be part of such a large class. I really think they will have to hire some adjunct faculty to cover all of the staffing needed for this semester. We will lose students during the first year for various reasons, but it's still a very large number of students in the freshman class. By the way, have you noticed a bit of an overload in your classes?" Valery thought for a second before she replied.

"I did have to take my swimming class in the evening because all the morning classes were full. It didn't bother me though, because since I don't know how to swim, it will be less frightening to take it with a smaller class.

"I see. Have you had any other problems?" Professor Brown had hoped that Valery would not be a target by the professors or the students because of her dark complexion. He would make a point of sharing whatever he knew about Valery to other professors if asked. He, however, wasn't as popular as he had once been by his peers since he now spent more time trying to help students with problems they had with administrative issues, and grievances with peers. He had even sided with several students when they had come to him with legitimate complaints about other professors. Behind his back, he was referred to as "brown nose, Brown." It didn't seem to bother him because he was focused on his job responsibilities and didn't have time to play the immature games that some of the faculty members played. He never had time to socialize with them so it didn't matter what they said.

"When was the last time you spoke with your sister, Valery?"

"I talked with her before I left New York. I really haven't had a chance to since I got back. Perhaps I can call her this weekend from the dorm whenever the telephone is free."

"Have you heard from Jolene?"

"Not this week, but she usually calls her mother once or twice a month. We encourage her to write more, but sometimes she says that she just wants to hear the sound of our voices. It's all right with me either way.

"Why don't you come over this weekend and bring your roommate Charlene?"

We'll cook up a little something and decide whether you two are going to make it here at Blue Keyes State or not." Valery smiled knowing Professor Brown was only joking with her.

"It's fine with me. I'll ask Charlene and see if she can come too. Thanks for the invitation." Professor Brown glanced at the clock on the wall which made Valery look too.

"Oops. Almost time for dinner. I promised to meet Charlene at the dining hall. I'd better go but I just wanted to drop by to say hello."

"Mrs. Brown and I will look forward to seeing you Saturday around five o'clock."

13

Dinner was really good but Valery and Charlene cautiously kept up with the time. Most of the freshmen had received notes under their dorm doors and were told to spread the word around. At six twenty that evening, most of the freshmen who were in the dining hall made an exit for the door and hurried to the back of the gym where they were met by at least one hundred upperclassmen. They were told to sit quietly and listen. The first to speak was a huge linebacker named Lester.

"I'm glad to see you all out here to support us. I know that some of you don't really understand why you're here. Well, let me begin by saying we all love our school and we all know that just going to school is a real special opportunity. We work hard on the football field trying to win games for you and to provide Blue Keyes State with the kind of reputation that will make you all proud." Lester acted as if he wasn't used to speaking publicly. He cleared his throat loudly into the microphone.

"I'll get to the point. We would like to have a Miss Blue Keyes State College that looks like the majority of us on this campus for a change. The young freshmen listened attentively and even began to murmur softly to each other. Another young upperclassman named Leon stepped forward. He was tall with very fair skin and equally handsome. When he began to speak, all sound was silenced as his very utterance commanded your attention.

"Students of Blue Keyes State College, we are here to set a wrong right. It has taken us a long time to get where we are today. Many a man had to lay down his life for the right to attend a college of any kind. It should be the right of every student here at Blue Keyes State College to vote for the 'Miss' of their choice. But vote for a "Miss" that holds dear the high standards put forth by the founders for this great institution. Vote for a "Miss" because she has a brain and uses it for things of importance. We don't want just another pretty face. We want an intellectually charming woman who is as beautiful on the inside as she is on the outside. A young lady that exemplifies the spirit of the Negro. Patient. Loving and kind. A young woman whose face is etched with the hope of tomorrow's dignity that is often denied us today. We need someone who can speak out on the issues that confront our people. Our Negro soldiers are fighting as we speak in a war against people that they don't even know and who have done nothing to us collectively as Negroes. We put our lives on the line for a country that refuses to even acknowledge us as equals. We can't go to the same schools or even attend the same churches for fear of our very lives. Hundreds of soldiers are at the forefront of this atrocity and we must stand behind them even on issues of this significance. If we don't stand up for what's right now, we never will!" Leon beckoned for someone. From among the crowd emerged a brown-skinned girl who looked pensively at the crowd of students. She found her place beside Leon. He then continued to address the "all ears" group of freshmen.

"Freshmen, we need your help! If you take a stand and vote for Beverly Steward, you'll help free this college of systemic colorism. Take a stand against the status quo! Take a stand for equality within our own race! You don't have to believe me, talk to Beverly and get to know her for yourselves. If you believe she has the integrity to not only make you proud, but to be a strong mentor for all college students of Blue Keyes State College, then vote for Beverly Steward! You freshmen are significant to this election. You have the power to make the change. Show your power in your vote! You can and will long be remembered as the freshman class of 1941 that broke the cycle of colorism. You will be the freshman class that had the guts to make the difference! Do it today…" When Leon finished speaking the freshmen began to clap moderately at first but then with fervor as they realized if everyone voted for Beverly Steward, it could change the trajectory of future Homecoming Queens. Leon was not only a brilliant speaker but also extremely charismatic. Even Valery and Charlene clapped. Lester stepped back in front of the freshmen and raised his hands at the crowd willing them to come back to order.

"I know that it's been hard for some of you since you've been on probation. I, too, was once a freshman and although I didn't experience most of the humiliation that many of you have, I did see some of my best friends endure punishments that were not fair. Now if you didn't know, the student government association is committed to keep our next 'Miss Blue Keyes State' as lily as the drippings of snow. However based on current student enrollment by classification, if all freshmen vote for Beverly Stewart, she will win by a slim margin but she will win! You'll get several notes under your doors in the next few weeks encouraging you to vote for Janice Holly Jones, 'their' pick for Homecoming Queen. Some of the notes will even ask you to meet with members of the student government staff in an attempt to influence your vote for Janice Holly Jones. Do not let them know your intentions. Play their game, however, what you do the day of the election is of your own choosing. If Beverly is elected, the entire football and basketball team along with some of the Greek organizations will petition to end your probation." The last words of the football player's speech were the words that every freshman wanted to hear.

"If we win, to celebrate, we'll have a bonfire and burn all the dog tags and beanies, and ladies, you can resume wearing your makeup." Cheers and shouts rang out as the freshmen left the meeting.

14

Valery and Charlene slept late Saturday. After they bathed and dressed, Charlene went to the library while Valery decided to walk down the campus to the Brown's cottage. As usual Mae Belle Brown greeted Valery with a warm hug.

"I was hoping you'd come over early. Where's your roommate?"

"She said she'd try to come, but she had to go to the library and if she completed her work in time, she'd meet me here." Mrs. Brown walked over to the oven to check her pot roast. She had decided to try a new recipe that called for placing your vegetables right in the pan with the beef roast and it would be done at the same time. She thought that was a good idea because it saved time and freed three burner rings. This way she could cook additional dishes. She knew that her husband liked potatoes and carrots, and she liked corn and broccoli. Valery like potatoes and corn so she could satisfy everybody's taste buds. The aroma from the kitchen was tantalizing and Valery couldn't wait until dinner.

The library was always such a cold place to Charlene. She also thought it was too quiet but it was the best place to get her work done. She didn't have to worry about anyone knocking on her door asking to borrow anything or being disturbed. Valery had encouraged Charlene to use the library as much as possible. Charlene had been there since early afternoon. She was doing research on Chaucer and the Canterbury Tales. She had read the story within a story and decided that Chaucer was indeed a real dreamer. Charlene was deep in thought when she heard the sound of someone speaking closely to her ear.

"I remember seeing you the other day in the dining hall during dinner. I also saw you at the rally behind the gym. I'm a freshman too. My name is Sidney." Charlene looking up from her notes to see a fresh face staring down at her. It had not occurred to her to invite him to sit down at the table but he did anyway.

"I've been working on a paper for English 101. My assignment was to do some research on the Canterbury Tales. I guess I should have gone to the library yesterday when my last class ended, but I thought I'd wait until today. Now I realize how much I don't know about Geoffrey Chaucer."

"I wish I could help you, but literature was never my favorite subject. I'm an engineer major. I grew up building toy bridges and designing buildings out of whatever I could find around the house. My brothers used to laugh at me and call me a sissy because I wouldn't play football with them or chase the girls. It didn't bother me much and I just kept building. When we did projects to turn in for homework in science, I would bring in some of my buildings. My science teacher was impressed and encouraged me to continue. I did and here I am."

"That's an interesting story. Where did you say you were from?"

"I didn't. But my hometown is Baton Rouge, Louisiana. I know where you're from already. I saw your dog tags."

"And where are your tags? You know that if you're caught without them, we'll have to be on probation a lot longer.

"Don't worry. I have them right here." Sidney stood up and reached into his pocket and pulled them out. I guess I forgot to put them back around my neck. By the way, how long are you planning to be here in the library?"

"Until I finish, I guess. Well, at least a couple of hours." Sidney stood up and quietly pushed his chair back in its place.

"If you're here when I finish my research, I'll walk with you back to the dining hall if that's where you're headed." Charlene was beaming with joy inside but managed to stay reserved outwardly.

"I'll think about it." She was determined not to look at Sidney as he walked away. She pulled Chaucer's book close to her and was lost in thought until Sidney returned later that afternoon, Charlene smiled as he approached and said she was ready to go. They made small talk on their way to the dining hall and it wasn't until halfway through the dinner meal that Charlene remembered she was supposed to have met Valery at the Brown's for dinner. The only thing that made her feel better about it was that she'd told Valery that if she didn't finish her research in time that she would not be able to come. She knew that everyone would assume as much and she would explain to Valery later. Dinner in the dining hall that evening was much better than it normally was but Charlene really wasn't paying that much attention to what it was that she was eating. Afterwards, Sidney and Charlene continued talking about everything they could think of.

15

"Thanks again Mrs. Brown. The food was delicious as usual. I hope that one day I'll be able to cook half as well as you do."

"Thank you for saying such nice things, Valery. I love having you around you know. I guess since Jolene has been away in New York, I haven't had anyone to spoil. Don't forget to take your pie and get one for your roommate. I hope you'll enjoy them."

"I'm sure we will. Goodbye now." Valery walked slowly toward the dorm thinking about the lovely evening she had with the Brown's. She still missed her mother and father a great deal but she didn't cry about them anymore. Her thoughts often drifted to the days she shared with them growing up. It was not until she heard the voice of a somewhat familiar voice that she looked up.

"Hey, you there freshman! Don't forget to vote for Janice Jones in the election on tomorrow. Remember, we can make it hard for you if you don't." Valery was not one to start trouble and decided to just wave and keep going. It didn't matter what they said to her about voting. She could vote for whomever she wanted and she had decided that Lester and Leon were right. Although she figured Janice was probably a nice enough candidate, when she browsed through the yearbooks that were on Professor Brown's coffee table, the one thing all "Miss Blue Keyes State College" queens had in common was their hue. The more she thought about it, the more she wondered why this was the case year after year.

Valery had known what it was like to be a dark-skinned girl. Her family and friends had chided her at times but always in a friendly way. At her high school, she was seen as a sort of heroine because of her athletic prowess so her darkness was not to her disadvantage. On tomorrow, she would support Beverly Stewart for two reasons. She was determined to be a part of major change in the way people looked at Miss Blue Keyes State College and because if Beverly did win, Lester and Leon would have to live up to their promise and let them off probation which would become an historical event. It would be hilarious to see the faces of the pompous governing body if it happened. A rare smile came across Valery's face as she put the key in her door, careful not to drop her pies, and unlocked it. Tomorrow would indeed be a good day.

16

John-Claude Adams was the son of Beatrice Adams. He was the older of two male children in the Adams family. Throughout his life, he had always been very meticulous. It was a trait his parents instilled in him early in his life. As he grew, his mother never had to remind him to hang up his clothes or clean up his room. He was a smart boy in school but he had never had many friends. As a matter of fact, other than a boy whose mother used to come over to the Adams' house to routinely borrow sugar and share any gossip she had heard from the neighbors, John-Claude never spent much time with other children. During his time in high school, he always made A's and took pride in sharing his knowledge of history with his classmates. He won numerous awards for competing against other schools in scholarly activities in the area of history and debate. When he graduated from high school, John-Claude received special permission from the school board to teach history in the school where he had once attended. News of his scholarliness in history had preceded him and he was honored to teach. He was paid nearly as much as the teachers and was often called on to give impromptu speeches when school board members visited the school and at nearby churches. He loved reading books about history and after teaching three years, he decided to attend college and learn all he could about historical events and how they connected to the present and the future. He was fascinated with the dates and names of famous people who made significant contributions to the world. Many men had died pioneering the land, championing causes, and many more would give their lives before political change would be made possible.

John-Claude had finally saved enough money to pursue his dream of going to college and adding to his cadre of knowledge. His life seemed to be directed and he thought he knew exactly what would happen. It had come as a tremendous shock when he turned 21 and received a letter from the New York Draft Board. John-Claude had read about the 1940 Conscription Law that had been the first ever to be in existence while the United States was at peace. It was technically called the Selective Training and Service Act. The law allowed for an annual induction of 900,000 men between the ages of 21 and 36. Ms. Adams had picked up the mail that day and when John-Claude got home, there were two letters laying on the small night stand in his bedroom. He was hoping to hear from one of the colleges to which he had applied. He tore open the first letter and was pleasantly surprised that not only had he been accepted, but he also had received a scholarship for all four years because his marks were so high. He clutched the letter to him and kissed it, thanking God for such a wonderful blessing. He started out of his room to tell his mother the good news. As he lay the letter down, his eyes caught the sight of the return address of the second letter marked 'New York Draft Board, Division 3487. John-Claude didn't want to believe what he was seeing. He balled his fist and held it to his lips, not believing that joy and pain could come to him simultaneously like this. He tore the envelope slowly, slipped the letter out and unfolded it. The message simply stated,

Dear Mr. Adams,

This letter is to inform you that on July 16, 1941, you are to report to the New York Draft Board to receive further instructions on your service to the United States Army Corp. You will need to bring the following items with you: A copy of your birth certificate and your social security card. You will consider this your final notice. Any attempt to disregard this notice or failure to comply with the above request will result in failure to perform duties required by the United States of America punishable by a minimum of five years.

The United States of America

John-Claude's mother didn't take the news well at all. He tried to comfort her, but she insisted they go to the draft board and contest the letter since he was a school teacher and all.

"It wouldn't matter mother, you have another son. It would only apply if I was an only child." He lied when he told her that it would be all right. She stopped crying when he said that going to fight for the country would give him a chance to see the world and add to his history background He tried to show her how important it would be to his future to not only share his knowledge from a book, but to also teach from real life experiences.

17

John-Claude's departure time was only a few week away and he struggled to get everything in order before he left. He spent the time before leaving his Brooklyn home writing a letter of resignation to the school board, his associates, and to the students that had grown to admire his teaching abilities. When it was time to leave New York, John-Claude tried desperately to keep a happy look on his face as his mother drove him to the recruiter's office. Recruits were to be dropped off at the front entrance with no parking. John-Claude gave his mother a final hug and kiss, quickly retrieved his luggage and headed to the door. It had been an arduous task making sure he had everything needed for the next six weeks that would be spent in a boot camp somewhere in Virginia. His mother had packed lots of chicken and bread and cookies for him to take on the journey. His stop at the recruitment office would be a matter of acquiring important information so that all his personal information would be on file. John-Claude began talking to the uniformed officer but the sergeant was not interested. They were seated in a small room with only a desk and two wooden chairs. The officer introduced himself as Sergeant Mayhill in traditional military nature.

"Speak when you are spoken to! Is that clear?"

"Yes sir."

"Until you get on that bus for Virginia, I'm your mama, your daddy, and anything else you need. Do you understand?"

"Yes sir." John-Claude had heard these kind of men were dogmatic in nature and if they thought you were intimidated by them in any way, it would be worse for you.

"Your name?"

"John-Claude Adams, sir"

"Where you from boy?"

"Brooklyn Heights, sir." John-Claude knew that even though the sergeant chose to call him boy, he must not let him know he resented it for fear of retaliation. The sergeant looked up from his desk and over his black horn-rimmed glasses and then decided to ask more questions. If he had enough sense to say 'yes sir' to him without him reading him the riot act, just maybe, this one might do well in one of the Colored divisions.

"What is your occupation…what school…parents…" After a seemingly endless barrage of questions from the sergeant John-Claude was finally dismissed and told to go with another officer to a room to get undressed. It only took a minute to slip off his shirt and slacks, laying them over the chair that was in the corner of the small examining room. He wrapped the discolored hospital gown around him and waited for the doctor. Within minutes the medical officer appeared in the room and told John-Claude that he would be given a complete physical and would have to pass before being allowed to enter the armed forces. In a way he hoped they would find something wrong with him, but he knew they wouldn't.

The officer, dressed in his sterile lab jacket, weighed John-Claude, measured his height and checked his eyes and nose, and told him to open his mouth wide. He also measured the width of his shoulders and took measurements that made John-Claude think that the information was being sought so he could be issued uniforms. The exam went on for at least twenty more minutes until finally the officer requested that he bend over. Not knowing what to expect, John-Claude did as he was told. It was pure instinct having someone invade him in such crude manner that he voiced vehemence.

"What in the hell are you doing?" John felt as if he had been violated.

"All done." The doctor looked unemotional as he responded.

"We check all recruits to make sure they are clean and not smuggling anything inside their bodies before they are sent to boot camp for training." With John's ego deflated, he struggled to not say more to the doctor.

"You're clean. Get dressed and wait here for your issue of clothing and assignment." John-Claude waited for the next officer to return and he was issued standard army clothing and his assignment. He stayed in a camp tent at the Central Division and was told he and a group of fellow recruits would be leaving the next morning.

It had been a long day for John-Claude. After a brief meal with the other six recruits that would be leaving the next morning, he retreated to his bunk bed. That night, he thought about how quickly and abruptly his life had changed. He was glad he had been drafted instead of his brother Charles. He could imagine seeing his brother crying like a baby and he almost laughed when he recalled the many times growing up that Charles would bend the truth so he wouldn't get a spanking. With John-Claude gone, Charles would have to take on more responsibility around the house. He would also be forced to stop procrastinating about going to college and really look at the options for a livelihood available to him. Before he went to sleep that night, he prayed and asked God to help him through the next few months of his life. He prayed that the leaders who incited this war would reconcile and let the world be at peace. He prayed that the United States would not be overturned and that he could return to the life he was being forced to leave. Not remembering when he fell asleep, John-Claude woke up to the sound of a loud male voice demanding he and the five other men that he didn't know move.

"On your feet recruits. Be dressed and on the bus at 0600 hours." John knew that meant six o'clock in the morning. He also had read that boot camp was hard and would make a man out of you in about three weeks. The newspapers he read in the school library always showed soldiers handsomely dressed in their attire with rifles by their sides and an ever so slight smile on their faces. He had always wondered what he would look like in one but his curiosity would now become a reality. It only took him a few minutes to dress. First out of the tent, John-Claude was ready for whatever was about to take place. When the other recruits made their way, they were all told to board the 976 Enlistment Bus that was parked in the front of the building. The old gray bus reminded John-Claude of a mode of transportation for prisoners but he fought to think loftier thoughts and resigned himself to positivity. Once all the recruits were on board, the journey began. In less than twenty minutes, all of John-Claude's suspicions came true about the old gray bus. It sputtered and faltered for the last time sending billows of smoke high into the air. The bus driver used his two-way radio to dispatch the location of the bus back to headquarters and within the hour the young men were placed on a silver and blue trimmed Greyhound bus headed for Fort Story in Virginia Beach, Virginia. This bus was nearly full of civilians when the six new recruits came aboard. The other five recruits found seats fairly close to the front, but by the time John-Claude boarded the bus there was only one seat left. He had just enough time to put his two bags under his seat and sit down before the bus began to move. The man he sat beside was snoring so loudly, and the older lady seated in the next aisle over, closest to the window, leaned forward and shook her head. The young lady sitting beside the older lady and closest to him looked as if she had been crying but he acted as if he didn't even see her and just listened to the sound of the bus engine hum as it cruised down U.S. 1.

After about an hour of riding, John-Claude began to feel himself slip into a sense of tranquility. Although he didn't really want to go to sleep right then, he finally gave in and within minutes he was dreaming about teaching classes to soldiers while fighting in World War II.

18

Valery woke up earlier than usual and decided that she would get a quick bath and then wake Charlene. Today would be the day that the freshmen would see how much power they really had on the campus. Charlene had chosen what clothes she would wear the night before so it wouldn't take her long to prepare once Valery awakened her.

"Good morning." Charlene rubbed her eyes and sat up in bed. She had slept well but lightly.

"Good morning to you. I hope you slept well last night."

"Yes, I did and you know why." The girls looked at each other and sniggered softly. As the two were walking towards the dining hall for breakfast, there were signs of the day's election for the Homecoming Queen election everywhere. At breakfast, it felt like some sort of secret faction was about to take place. All of the freshmen were on time for breakfast and to emphasize the election day to elect the new 'Miss', the student government president made an announcement reminding everyone to vote just before the grace was sung. There was applause from all the students as Janice Holly Jones, the fair-skinned candidate, stood amidst the applause to acknowledge her expectation of majority vote. She waved to her constituents while Beverly Stewart sat demurely smiling and wondering if she had made a big mistake by running against tradition.

As the student waiters prepared to distribute platters of food to each table, Valery noticed Rodney Biggs, lumbering his way toward the empty seat at their table. His appetite was always voracious and he rarely cared about social mores. It took a few minutes before their table waiters arrived with a platters of eggs, grits, sausage, and toast. As soon as the platter of sausage left the waiters hands, Rodney immediately grabbed it and scraped half of them onto his plate, leaving only four sausage patties for the other seven people at the table to eat. Valery decided that she was in no hurry and would wait for the next platter of sausage to arrive. The platter with the grits had been placed on her side of the table. As she looked down at the white fluffy grits, she noticed something dark in the bowl and realized it was a brown kitchen roach. Charlene saw it too. Rodney was busy chopping up his sausage patties and asking if someone would pass the grits. Valery readying to tell him that there was a bug in the food but stopped when Charlene elbowed her in the rib cage signaling her to be quiet. Charlene reached pass Valery and proudly passed the grits to Rodney who never looked down as he spooned several serving of grits, roach included, into his chopped up sausage patties. Without knowing the roach was there, Rodney ate heartily consuming everything on his plate. Valery felt nauseated but Charlene began laughing softly, then more loudly until the cafeteria manager came out and asked her to stop or leave the dining hall. Charlene left with Valery following right behind her.

For the rest of the day, students found time between their classes and meals to go to the gym where the voting booths were set up. There were students designated from both Janice and Beverly's campaign to make sure that no one did anything illegal. The voting closed at five o'clock that afternoon giving all participants an opportunity to vote for the 'Miss' of their choice. All votes would be lock up and tallied the next day. Since no one was sure who had keys to the room where the ballots were being housed, both campaign managers decided that they would take turns posting someone from their headquarters to stand guard outside the door all night.

The next day, by noon, the votes were counted and the final tally revealed the winner. For the first time in the history of the school, the new Miss Blue Keyes State College was Beverly Steward, darkly-pigmented, intelligent, and proud that she had achieved with the help of the freshmen class, the distinct honor of representing Blue Keyes State. The upperclassmen demanded a recount of the votes and even President Lee was concerned. He called a meeting with the student government president to discuss the matter. When Steven Cook arrived, the president's secretary told him to go right on in.

"Steven. Please sit down." Steven had been caught off guard by the results of the election and was uneasy not knowing what President Lee would say.

"Yes, sir. How are you today sir?" President Lee was in no mood for small talk and got right to the point...

19

The freshmen students wore their beanies and dog tags proudly for the rest of the week. On Saturday morning, there was a note under every freshman's door. The note read:

To All Freshmen
At 8:00 tonight, you are invited to a special celebration. Don't forget to wear your probation paraphernalia. Be on time!
Leon and Lester

Still reeling from the election results, the upperclassmen requested a recount that was honored but changed nothing. The freshmen and supporters of Beverly Steward on the other hand were thrilled, looking forward to the promise made them to burn the dog tags and beanies. Many were hopeful to be able to wear a little make-up after tonight instead of putting it on in the cloak of their bathroom suites, and washing it off every morning before going to class.

As the evening approached, more and more freshmen were seen leaving Frazier Hall headed in the direction of the gym. Word and rumors of an early probation release had reached the ear of Steven Cook. This terrified him as President Lee had given a stark warning of the loss of revenues Blue Keyes State could face from big business supporters if adherence to their requests were not followed. Steven had to take action. Ten minutes before eight o'clock nearly all freshmen had assembled behind the gymnasium.

Some of the girls who were more than ready to be alleviated of the disgusting probationary measures were already wearing makeup. Valery met Charlene there and placed their dog tags, beanies, and placards outside amongst the pile that had already accumulated. At exactly eight o'clock both Leon and Lester appeared. At the very sight of the two young men, the freshmen began clapping. The two men held their hands and the crowd fell silent. Leon was the first to speak.

"Today signals the first day of an historical moment for Blue Keyes State College. As the freshmen class of 1941, you have done something that has never been achieved before. You have listened to your inner hearts and souls and sought to change the course of an unfair standard that has been practiced her for many, many years. For the first time, this institution of education will be reflective of its majority population. It is important to know that Beverly Steward will still have many barriers to overcome, but we will be there to support her. If she is not invited to the luncheons that her predecessors have attended we will stand in protest. We will make sure that she is shown respect by all. If she is not be called on to speak and travel with the administration, as has been the tradition, we will protest. We will demand that she be allowed to represent the voice of our student body and not be intimidated to simply reiterate meaningless words. She will share new and bold ideas that will usher in fairness for all students regardless of color. And now, I would like for each of you to meet Miss Blue Keyes State College, Beverly Steward." Beverly stepped out and was greeted with shouts of adoration by the freshmen, a number of Greeks, the football team, and a few upperclassmen who had heard about the meeting. Beverly raised her hand and immediately the crowd hushed.

"I would like to thank each of you for having the courage to believe that we could win. I haven't had a chance to be congratulated by President Lee, but there was a note in my mail box that said he was truly happy that I had been chosen." There were a few murmurs made from the crowd but she continued.

"As I promised you, I will do everything within my power to see to it that you as freshmen, as well as all other students on this campus are treated fairly and with respect. It will not be business as usual for some and the leftovers for others. We will work to ensure that all students are given the same opportunities and if you need anything, please contact me. You know that I am always ready to listen to your needs. Thank you and again…" Valery couldn't hear the last sentence Beverly said because the applause was deafening. She could not have been more proud of Beverly. Her courage inspired her and she hoped to one day feel that same courage when she completed all her course work and was ready to leave Blue Keyes State College, as a graduate, ready to join the professional work force. It was now Lester's time to speak to the freshmen. As he raised his hand the students once again silenced themselves.

"I know this is the moment you have all been waiting for. We promised you that if you voted for Beverly, she would win. And she did win. I also promised you that if she won Leon and I would personally see to it that you no longer would be on probation. Well, we're men of our words. So as of today…" Lester's voice trailed off as Steven Cook leapt onto the make shift platform, determined to denounce what he feared Lester was about to say.

"As your student government president, I declare this an illegal meeting. If you do not disperse immediately, I will call campus police. Your activities will be reported to President Lee and you may be expelled from Blue Keyes or even worse arrested! A six-week probation has been a part of the freshman tradition for decades. Its purpose, much to the dismay of my uninformed colleagues here, is to provide a way for the freshmen to be known to the upperclassmen in an expedient manner. If it weren't for the placards, dog tags, and beanies that you wear, how in the Name of God would we ever get to know you? Now, you have already been on probation for a month. In a few short weeks, providing no one else does anything stupid and gets the whole lot of you thrown out, you will all be free to walk around like everyone else. To help you, I am willing to pretend this never happened. Now I suggest you pick up your beanies, dog tags, placards, adjourn this meeting and go back to your dormitories." Lester began to chant.

"Oh, no, we won't go." Lester began to chant. The chanting began softly until Lester stepped back in front of Steven and encouraged the chanting to continue. Steven Cook was livid but he left the stage as the football players pressed their way to the front to prevent anyone else from further disturbing the meeting. Lester was now in control and shouted, "Burn 'em" before he handed the torch to one of the football players to start the bonfire that would forever be known at Blue Keyes as the Bonfire of 1941.

20

John-Claude had enjoyed the bus ride and especially talking to the young lady he met named Valery Lewis. He could sense there were insecurities behind the strong personality she attempted to portray to him. Perhaps she thought he would say something to her that was out of line so she launched the first missile by letting him know she was not the easy going type. John-Claude had been impressed by her knowledge far out-weighing that of most of the high schoolers he taught at Brooklyn Heights High. He thought if he had let her know he was a teacher himself, she would not have spoken so freely. Too, he was amused at her ability to hold an intellectual conversation. He watched her fall asleep on the bus in the early morning hours even though she never knew it. Blue Keyes State College was where she was headed for the next four years of her life and he wished her well. He and the other five recruits emerged from the bus and hurriedly made their way to the last connecting bus that would take them to Fort Story.

John-Claude's legs had stiffened and he was relieved to get off the bus to get the blood circulating in his legs and arms. As he did, he looked into the faces of the other recruits he had met. Collins, Wilson, Kapeheart, Milner, and Smith were their last names. Of the six men, one was probably the most shattered to have received the draft order. Ronnie Kapeheart had been studying to become a lawyer. He was from a very prominent Negro family living in Long Island. Wanting the family business to continue to grow, his father fought through the legal system to keep his son out of the draft but Uncle Sam was determined and in the end Ronnie had to leave his parents. He was very angry that his life had been interrupted by Uncle Sam and he let everyone around him know it. Soon they boarded the bus for the last connection to Fort Story.

After another five hours of riding the Greyhound the bus finally stopped. It was in front of a long, gray building that reminded John-Claude of what a prison must resemble. A man dressed in military attire came on the bus shouting loudly for the men to exit. John-Claude grabbed his things and exited as did everyone else on the bus except Kapeheart. The officer jumped on the bus and ran down the bus aisle until he was inches from Kapeheart's face. Kapeheart didn't expect the officer to be so abrupt and it must have scared his nonchalant attitude to one of wide-eyed wonder. He moved with the drill sergeant on his heels. Now the six men stood outside the bus as the drill sergeant began issuing orders.

"Welcome to Virginia Beach men. I am your drill sergeant. You may call me Sergeant Gobar. While in my command you will do as all superior officers tell you. Is that clear?" The soldiers lowered their heads and said 'yes sir'.

"You now belong to the United States. We are responsible for everything you need. You will rise and shine each morning bright and early. Do you understand?"

By the end of the evening, the six men joined the other fifty or so colored soldiers that had come from the northeastern part of the country. After being shown how to correctly make their bunk beds, they reported to the mess hall for dinner. They went through the line choosing a meat that resembled meatloaf, lumpy potatoes, cold green beans, and a glass of water. The two found seats at one of the cafeteria styled tables. John-Claude paused before eating to give God thanks while Kapeheart grabbed his fork and dug in. The food wasn't too bad but it lacked seasoning and tasted bland. Kapeheart, sitting right beside John-Claude made a point of saying so too loudly. One of the military sergeants on duty overheard him complaining about it and both he and John-Claude were ordered from the table and taken outside. Although the military police knew who had made the comment, it was his way to teach Kapeheart that when one suffered all could suffer. To punish them, Sergeant Gobar placed the two men on guard duty for the night with empty stomachs. They were warned if they were caught sleeping, it would mean guard duty around the clock. John-Claude waited until the sergeant was out of earshot before he spoke.

"What in the world were you thinking when you decided to open your big mouth and end not only your supper but mine as well?" John-Claude was visibly irritated and decided it was time to say something.

"You must understand by now that nothing is going to be as it was back home. We are from the same area and these hicks probably have never set foot outside Virginia. Don't you realize that we are being targeted and if you don't keep your mouth shut, we may lose more than just a meal?"

Kapeheart looked as though he could break every bone in John-Claude's body then stared straight ahead for several moments before he spoke.

"I know my rights around here. If they expect me to risk my tail for them they could at least feed me a decent meal. Did you taste that mess?" John-Claude could truly understand how Kapeheart felt but it would do him more harm than good to speak about the treatment he or anyone else was getting. After all, this was wartime. For the rest of the evening the two men calmed down and got to know each other.

At first it wasn't so bad walking around the barracks standing guard. John-Claude found out that Kapeheart preferred to be called 'Kape', a nickname given him by the boys in his neighborhood. However, by two o'clock in the morning, Fort Story grew quiet as the veil of the previous evening permeated throughout their bodies making their eyes weary.

"Man, I'm gonna sit down and rest my bones for a minute." John-Claude was tired too, but he feared any repercussion by the drill instructor and warned Kape not to do it. Kape thought about a way they both could survive the rest of the night.

"I'll tell you what. Let's take turns. You keep walking around for about thirty minutes and then wake me up. I'll walk for thirty minutes so you can doze and I'll wake you. Deal? Come on Mr. School Teacher. I know you're tired too.

Though unsure, John-Claude reluctantly agree to Kape's terms not because he thought it was a good idea, but because it was ludicrous for both of them to have to stand up and walk around the barracks all night. The first hour worked well and they had both had sufficient naps. When it was John-Claude's turn to get his thirty minute nap, Kape felt sure that no one would be coming at three o'clock in the morning checking on them. John-Claude, being a light sleeper heard the barrack door open and spotted the drill instructor coming toward them. John-Claude rose slowly and crept through the bushes until he reached the back of the barracks and quickly rubbed his eyes trying to appear more alert than he really was. Where was Kape and why had he not awakened him? The answer came just as he finished the thought.

"Well, what have we here? Private Kapeheart, you were commanded to guard your post. If this had been real enemy territory we could all have been killed because you weren't man enough to assume your responsibilities. And where is Private Adams?"

"Here sir!"

"Have you been asleep like your buddy here?" John-Claude looked at Kape and wanted to tell the truth but the truth could only have hurt them both. John-Claude had already been punished enough thanks to Kape's big mouth.

"No sir!" John-Claude instinctively knew that Kape had decided to take a nap during his time to patrol instead of guarding the barracks and keeping an eye out for the Sergeant Gobar and now he would have to pay.

"Good job, Private Adams, you're relieved from duty. You've got time for about forty winks. Your buddy here has had all the sleep he's going to need for a while." John-Claude walked quickly toward the barracks avoiding Kape's insolent glare.

21

"Rise and shine, privates! Today is going to be a day to remember. I expect you to be in formation at 0500 hours. You won't disappoint me will you?" Before Sergeant Gobar left the barracks, he strode past John-Claude's bunk and winked his eye as if to say he had punished Kape justifiably for falling asleep during his watch. After he left, the soldiers began to sleepily fall out of their bunks and get dressed. John-Claude didn't feel refreshed at all but knew that he'd better try to look as alert as all the other privates.

At exactly 0500 hours, all soldiers were front and center, ready for whatever action was about to take place. Sergeant Gobar stood tall and still as the soldiers positioned themselves in straight lines. He suspected that this would be perhaps one of the finest battalion's he would ever train. He had looked at the profiles of the men and was impressed at their educational backgrounds. They had come from good homes and some of the men had fathers who had served in previous wars. They had strong examples for leaders at home and he knew that only a few would need to be broken. Private Kapeheart's profile fit the description of one who would need to be strictly disciplined. He was a typical spoiled brat who unfortunately had been drafted. Sergeant Gobar would need to punish him effectively to make certain that he could be counted on if his platoon ever needed him. Sergeant Gobar knew all too well that error in judgement could cost lives. His men had to be particularly focused and precise. He had been subjected to much criticism during his eighteen years of service in the military. If trained properly, he saw no reason why a Negro battalion would be denied the right to fight as soldiers and not be given the same duties and respect as his White counterparts. When the occasion arose, Sergeant Gobar's men would prove to be the most valuable men serving in the United States Army, and one day he might be rewarded for all his hard work. Sergeant Gobar, joined by his staff, faced the platoon.

"This morning would have been a day of relaxation for you new recruits, but last night one of your comrades fell asleep while on duty leaving you all vulnerable to the enemy. If one soldier makes a mistake, we all could die. The soldier is being disciplined as we speak. Let this be a hint to the wise. Never disobey an order or you will suffer the consequences. And as a reminder, we will forego breakfast today and begin our training. Since your canteens are already full and packed, let's move 'em out."

The grueling regiment that day was exhausting. Some recruits tried to be considerate when a comrade was in need of something if the sergeant wasn't looking, though that did not happen often. Sergeant Gobar seemed to be everywhere at all times. By noon, the whole squad was so bedraggled that many of the men were too tired to eat. John-Claude tried to pace himself throughout the day, stopping only to take quick sips of water and keep his breathing as evenly as possible. He had thought about Kape off and on that day, wondering what type of punishment he had endured.

Kape was sound asleep on his bunk when John-Claude returned to the barracks. He tried to wake him for lunch, but Kape seemed to be somewhat incoherent. Perhaps he had been allowed food before he went to sleep. John-Claude joined the other recruits and was thankful to have food. The meal was good considering that he hadn't eaten for two days. Afterwards, the recruits were given the rest of the day off. Later that evening, John-Claude tried to awaken Kape again. He groaned heavily as he rolled over and grabbed at his side.

"What happen to you, man?" The look on Kape's face was worth a thousand words, but his response was simple.

"Get out of my face. What the hell do you care?" John-Claude lowered his voice as he spoke to Kape, hoping he would be understanding.

"You were supposed to be walking. When I woke up, I barely had time to get to my feet and walk around to you before he would have seen me asleep too. Why didn't you at least wake me up before you decided to play the odds against the middle? John-Claude could tell Kape was still angry but he was also in pain.

"I never asked to be here and I won't be treated like an animal. I'll bet white soldiers aren't treated the same way we are. If I ever get out of here, I'm filing a law suit against the sergeant and Uncle Sam. The pain in Kape's side was beginning to ache even more and he wondered if he had a broken rib.

22

When John-Claude was dismissed to back to the barracks in the wee hours of the morning, Sergeant Gobar ordered Kape to stand guard for the rest of the night. At first, Kape stayed awake from the adrenaline that was pumping through him at the shock of being caught, but after a while, his body was barely able to put one foot in front of the other. The sergeant was fully awake and sat down on a grassy mound nearby to observe. On several occasions when Kape slumped to the ground, the sergeant would get up, go over to him, and yell at him that the enemy was coming and that he had to save the squad. After another hour passed, Kape collapsed, falling hard to the ground, but the sergeant was relentless. Using his baton, he poked Kape in his side, arousing him but Kape did not get to his feet. If he had, the sergeant would have believed Kape was willing to sacrifice himself for his fellow comrades, but he made no further attempt.

The disciplining of a recruit always made Sergeant Gobar sick but it was a necessary evil. He realized that this war was no place for young Private Kapeheart. He had come from a family that used words and the legal system to achieve success but it made no difference in war. Disciplining him was the best thing he could do to help him survive. The beating had been swiftly executed and afterwards he was taken to the infirmary where he stayed while the rest of the recruits were out in the field training. Kape would be fine physically and the sergeant hoped this would be the end of his insolence. Kape's description of what had taken place with the sergeant sounded harrowing. John-Claude tried to listen without hating the sergeant but it seemed like such a rotten thing to do to someone. He would help Kape if he could. He started by getting him some food. By early evening the word spread about Kape and what would happen if any other recruits were caught disobeying the commands of an officer in charge. Fear soon turned to distrust among the men and everyone began to look out for themselves. In time, Kape's body healed and he trained under the watchful eye of the sergeant. After six weeks, the men had completed their training. Sergeant Gobar had turned the men into a fine squadron ready for combat. On November 30, 1941, the 42nd Army Infantry was flown in military planes to Guam.

23

Valery had finished her first semester as a college student at Blue Keyes State College. The coldness of winter had snuggled around the campus grounds. Snow covered the roofs and grass making it fun for snowball throwing. There were Greek made snowmen and the campus had been beautifully decorated. Her sister along with Jolene had come from New York to the campus for a visit. When Valery's last exam for the fall semester was completed, she nearly ran the entire way to the Brown's house knowing that Mary would be there when she arrived. To her surprise, Mary had purchased a bicycle that she could use to get around on the campus once winter was over. Some of the students, whose parents were financially well off, had cars. But that never bothered Valery.

She could hardly control her excitement. She was the proud owner of a bicycle that her sister had given her. She would use it to help her stay in shape.

"Thank you so much Mary."

"I hope you like it." Mary wanted to make sure Valery had some of the things she knew she wanted.

"I love it! How long are you all going to stay?" Valery wanted to know right away so she could plan to spend as much time as possible with her sister. She hoped Mary could stay for at least a week. That way, they could get caught up on all that had been happening in New York and still find time to meander around the city of Blue Keyes.

"As long as you want me to." Mary laughed as she reached over and gave her little sister a big bear hug. Mary had taken a week off from work. She had just been promoted to head cashier in the lingerie department at Macy's and was able to save some of the earnings with which she bought the bicycle. Mary had also shopped to find clothes she knew Valery would like. As a physical education major, Valery liked to dress in white. White slacks, white blouses, white socks, white shoes, white winter coat, and if she had chosen to carry a small handbag, it too would have been white. At times, some of the students would turn to watch her as she walked down the campus, snickering and sometimes calling her 'snowball'. She pretended she didn't hear them.

"I've really missed you squirt." Valery, Mary, and Jolene ran up the stairs and flung themselves on the guest bed laughing and enjoying having the people they loved most all in the same place at the same time.

"Squirt? Did I hear that correctly? You're beginning to sound like a mother hen but I do have something to show you." Valery slid off the bed and reached into the dresser drawer and pulled out the letter she had received from the college showing her grades for the semester.

Valery had been very proud of her semester grades, especially her chemistry grade. Professor Brown had given her the name of an astute young man who was doing his internship and was more than happy to share his knowledge with Valery. Dwight Smith was an energetic student who had spent a lot of time working with chemicals and their reactions in the school's science laboratory. On Tuesdays and Thursdays evenings after supper, Valery would meet with Dwight and watch him work in the chemistry lab. He talked to her about substances of matter, the investigation of properties and how they interacted, combined, and changed to form new substances. Although she was only an advanced freshman, she listened intently to him. He helped her understand the symbols for different chemicals and she often assisted him in his lab experiments. Sometimes Dwight would give her his key to the lab so she could practice on some of her experiments when she had time. He reminded her that only professors and interns were allowed access to the room that stored active chemicals. He also reminded Valery to take good care of the key so that neither of them would get in trouble. Dwight taught her how to mix sulfur and toxins. He told her how important it was to record her work so if by chance she discovered something of great importance, she would know how to recreate it. Her relationship with Dwight was purely plutonic even though she had a feeling he liked her. Valery's chemistry teacher was proud of the extra work that she obviously had done to always remain a step ahead of the rest of her class.

"Good grades. I am so proud of you!" Mary was happy to see that Valery had adapted to life as a college student. It had been a long time since she thought about the fact that in a few years, Valery would be finished with her college studies and ready for her first experience in the working world. She had always wanted life to be special for Valery. It would have been exactly what her mother and father would have wanted her to do. The three girls spent the rest of the week at the Brown's cottage. They talked on end about all of their goals and accomplishments. Jolene would be a junior when school began in the fall, and Mary was happy for her new promotion at Macy's.

Mrs. Brown had been out most of the day. Her church was having their annual winter festival. The children in the community and their parents would gather to offer thanks to God, decorate the pine tree the church had purchased, play games, visit with the elderly that were able to attend, and have an indoor holiday meal in the basement of the church. There was so much food the members divided the leftovers to take to their families. Mrs. Brown was glad she would not have to cook, that way, she could spend more time with her daughter, Valery and her older sister. She had never seen Mary before her arrival with Jolene and she was quite surprised at the difference in the complexion of the two. Mary was very pale and actually could have almost passed for white. Valery was, on the other hand just the opposite but it didn't take long for her to see that the colors of the two girls did not faze them. It was their love for each other that was striking. Mrs. Brown, home now, had just finished warming their supper.

"Girls. Come down. It's time to eat." The table was beautifully set and she put her best china and silverware on the table to commemorate the homecoming of her daughter and Mary. After washing their hands, the girls came downstairs laughing as they entered the kitchen. Jolene's eyes sparkled as she looked with pride at her mother's table. As their eyes met, she ran to her mother hugging and kissing her on the forehead. Mrs. Brown, trying to dismiss the feelings of melancholy she felt, waved her off. Mr. Brown's timing was perfect. He entered the house, put his briefcase down, kissed his wife and daughter, hugged Valery, and waited to be introduced to Mary.

"Professor Brown, this is my sister, Mary."

"Mary, this is Professor Brown." They both started to speak at once, they both stopped and started to speak at once again. Everyone began to laugh at the two. They both stopped trying to speak and just embraced each other.

"It's so good to finally meet the other half of Valery. It feels like I already know you."

"Me too." Mary was humbled by his graciousness and held back tears of joy. Mrs. Brown asked if anyone was ready to eat, to which she received four hearty yeses. After prayer, dinner began. The meal was delicious and the family moaned with delight as they tried to include at least one of the many desserts leftover from the winter festival. Everyone traded stories for a while, Mr. Brown excused himself from the table and headed to the living room area for his after a fabulous meal nap. The girls got up and helped Mrs. Brown clear the table and wash the dishes. That night, Jolene came into the bedroom and announced that her father would be sleeping on the couch, she would be sleeping with her mother so the two girls could have the upstairs bedroom.

24

The next morning when the girls woke up it was already 9:00. Valery was so used to getting up much earlier to go to breakfast in the dining hall and scurry off to her classes that she didn't realize how tired she was. She had been so excited about Mary's arrival and was definitely going to make the best of it. It had been decided that Mrs. Brown would take them all into town to do a little shopping and go to a movie. Breakfast smells began to infiltrate the upstairs bedroom. Mary awakened with a start.

"What's wrong?" Valery raised up in the bed to see if Mary was okay. Her sister looked around the room as if she was very confused and then buried her face in her hands.

"The kitchen smells reminded me of Mother. I must have been dreaming, because we were back home and she was calling us for breakfast." Valery knew Mary was caught off guard because she made a point to never mention their parents. It was understood that the accident was something neither of them would ever forget and talking about it could not bring them back.

"It's all right, Mary. I know how you feel. I still have dreams about them sometimes. I think that's one of the reasons that I am so attached to the Browns. They really remind me of mother and father. They seem to always be concerned with my well- being and how I'm doing in school. Professor Brown went out of his way when I first came here to make sure I had everything I needed. Sometimes I think he does too much not only for me but for many of the students here. I hear that some of the staff members are a little jealous of how he makes sure that students are being treated fairly. Mary turned to her sister.

"Sound like the Brown's are just what we needed, eh?" Mary and Valery got up, bathed and got dressed. Jolene was just coming to get them as they headed down the stairs.

"Good morning! So you two sleepy heads finally woke up. I thought we were going to have to sound the bugle for you." Valery yawned.

"I can't believe I slept this long, but I feel very refreshed." The girls walked into the kitchen as Mrs. Brown was putting butter on top of her golden brown biscuits.

"Good Morning girls. There are your plates. Serve yourselves. There's plenty of food to go around so eat 'til your heart's content'. Jolene insisted on helping me cook this morning. I thought you'd better know that, so make sure you say a good blessing before you eat.

"Mother."

"I'm just kidding. Now you know how well Jolene can cook. She started out when she was about seven years old. She'd get up early before everyone else and cut the old Victrola on. She'd grab an old mop or broom or whatever she could find and dance around 'til she got tired. Then she'd be all happy and out of breath and come into her father's and my room. She'd tap me ever so lightly on the shoulder until she woke me up. I'd open one eye and she'd ask me if I was awake. I'd try to ignore her but who could turn down a face like that. I'd get on up and the two of us would whip up griddle cakes, fresh sausage, fried green apples, and on some Saturday's I'd help her fix a batch of grits. Her father would wake up and come downstairs ready for breakfast and Jolene would hide his plate in the oven and tell him there was none left. He would make the saddest face that anyone could image and afterwards she would tell him it was just a joke. He'd grab her up and give her the biggest hug. He always knew I would never cook a meal and not make enough for him but he played along so she could get the big hug anyway." Jolene poured tall glasses of orange juice for everyone as they sat down. Mrs. Brown said the blessing and the girls truly felt blessed for having had the opportunity to eat it.

The day was cold but clear and beautiful outside. They saw several students from the college in town buying holiday gifts for their families. Mrs. Brown had driven them and they window shopped for about an hour, looking into every store front they saw. Mary enjoyed comparing clothes in Blue Keyes to the ones in New York district. Most of the clothes she saw were at least a season behind. It was interesting and she enjoyed sharing with them the difference in prices. They purchased some items and decided to talk about the movie they would attend.

"I hear Humphrey Bogart is playing in 'Casablanca'." Mary had remembered seeing his name on nearly every theater marquis in Harlem.

"I think he's a great actor. He played in a movie I saw last year. He's what some people call ruggedly handsome. Anyway, let's go."

Mrs. Brown purchased four tickets. She handed the tickets out to the girls and they all got in line with all the other moviegoers. As they inched their way inside, the usher who stood tall and stately looked casually at the patrons as they gave him their tickets. Mrs. Brown, who was at the front of the line, handed her ticket to the usher who simply said 'upstairs'. Valery and Jolene were also told 'upstairs,' but when Mary handed her ticket to the usher, he stepped to the side and said 'straight ahead'. Mary assumed that the usher could tell they were all together, but Mary made her position clear.

"I'm with them. Excuse me." The usher moved and simply looked the other way. Mrs. Brown, Valery nor Jolene reacted to the slight.

"How about the smell of that popcorn?" Mary said as she thought of a brilliant idea.

"Why don't I get the popcorn and hot chocolate for everyone? I'll meet you upstairs." Once they found their choice of seating in the upper tier of the theatre and settled in, the movie began. It was a love story about a group of refugees in Casablanca during World War II who were trying to find their way out while gathering at a watering hole called Rick's. It was a great movie and Valery thought the music was terrific. She hummed "I'm Singing in the Rain," all the way home. The girls had enjoyed their day with Mrs. Brown and tried to reward her by making her sit down while they cooked dinner for her although she contested the idea.

"I'll have none of this. Don't forget, I don't get a chance to spoil you often so let me enjoy this." Jolene hugged her mother, playfully kissing the top of her head as the three headed upstairs.

"Wasn't that movie simply divine?" They talked about everything from the newest records which included Artie Shaw, the King Cole Trio, Cab Calloway's Orchestra, and Fats Waller, to the latest hair styles, clothes, and accessories.

After the initiation of drafting men to serve in wars, time became more frightening. Newspapers and radios talked constantly of the bravery of young soldiers that volunteered to give their lives if it took that for the safety of their country. It was important because men were being drafted at an alarming rate. In 1939, the United States Selective Service had one hundred ninety thousand men at their disposal. However, the number was greatly expanded to more than two million men. The Selective Service Act of 1940 required all male citizens ages twenty one through thirty five to register for a year of military service. Valery secretly scoffed at the public accounts of heroism played out in hometown parades exclusive of the fact that these men had little choice as to whether they wanted to serve their country as a pawn in a game of chess or fulfill their own personal goals. She wished world leaders could come together and problem solve amicably the exchange of goods and services in ways that would benefit the nations instead of being greedy and causing confusion and war.

Mary too, had heard that lots of soldiers were being killed overseas. She thought about the recruit Valery wrote her that she had met on the bus on her way to Blue Keyes College. She felt sorry to him, knowing his chances for making it back home were slim. Mary looked at her younger sister who seemed to be growing up right in front of her eyes. Her once flat chest was no longer void of curves. She knew that taking physical education courses would enhance her figure but Valery was truly turning into quite a foxy young lady. She wondered if Valery had found a boyfriend yet. It had been a year since the two of them had seen each other so she wouldn't be too surprised. Valery had been watching her sister, and as if by mental telepathy, she could tell Mary wanted to ask her about her love life.

"Get that look off of your face, Mary. The answer is no. Absolutely not. There's no one." Mary looked at her for a moment before she mentioned her chemistry tutor.

"And how's Dwight, by the way? You do remember him, don't you? You know, the one who spends several hours in the chemistry lab with you each week and teaches you all about formulas. Come on girl, you can tell me. I'm your sister." Valery tried to hold her laughter inside but she couldn't.

"You've got to be kidding. Dwight is a very nice person but I'll not pretend that our relationship could ever be more than friendship. Actually, neither one of us has time to socialize, taking as many hours as we do." Jolene couldn't resist the temptation to tease her just a little more.

"What about that handsome recruit who rode with you part of the way to Blue Keyes College? Mary told me you thought he was cute. Did you two exchange addresses or anything like that?"

"No. For your information, I did say that he was very handsome. If I was interested in having a relationship, which I am not, John-Claude would be at the top of the list. But his training was over ten months ago and I have no idea where he is now." Mary liked seeing Valery's shyness and chided her one last time.

"I'll bet you wouldn't mind singing in the rain with him."

25

On November 30, 1941, a military plane carrying the Fort Story Platoon flew to army headquarters, Fort Shafter, Hawaii. The small island was actually located in the south end of the Marianas, about thirteen hundred miles east of the Philippines. It measured thirty miles long, and four to ten miles wide, covering an approximate two hundred nine square miles. John-Claude surveyed the land observing the coral reefs off its coast. There was a limestone plateau that arose on the northern part of the island. The forests were thick making much of the living obscure to most planes flying overhead. The southern part of the quaint tropical wonderment had mountain ranges of volcanic origin. There were several rivers that originated from the mountains which ran to the coast. The weather was quite warm, ranging in the low eighties unlike New York weather for that time of year. Most of the population were descendants of the island's original inhabitants and other Micronesia islanders. The women were particularly short in statue and had long, dark hair. The troops stayed there for two days and were then transported by boat to Antigua, Guam.

Guam was probably one of the best kept secrets in the Pacific. John-Claude had never really read a lot about the small tropical island although he knew that the United States had to protect all of the land that it possessed even if it was no larger than a pinhead on the map. The island was located in Micronesia in the Western Pacific Ocean. The men were warned upon arrival of the nature of the people and its inhabitants. They were also told of their boundaries and the consequences of not following orders. Colonial Williams, a short stocky Caucasian official from the 99th brigade was in charge of the squad along with many other commissioned and non-commissioned officers. Since the 42nd consisted of only Negro soldiers, they were mostly treated by white soldiers as if they were in servitude positions. It took a couple of fights before the men understood their best chance of survival was to function as a team. All came to the realization that one was no better than the other if a bomb exploded as they could be mortally wounded. John-Claude had come to appreciate the seemingly cruel treatment Sergeant Gobar inflicted on him and the fellow privates during training. They felt there was no problem insurmountable. They were ready to take on the Japanese and anyone else that stood in the way of peace for the United States. All the men were ready to get back to their families too. They wrote to their loved ones as often as possible, but it was never the same, knowing that whatever you wrote was being censured to make sure that no military secrets were being divulged. John-Claude had written letters to his mother and brother. He wondered how the high school students he tutored were doing and he occasionally addressed and sent a post card to the school address.

"Turn in early tonight men. Rumor has it that tomorrow may be a busy day." Lieutenant Colonel Bradford, the officer in charge of the division had always reminded John-Claude of a man who couldn't be trusted. He had only seen him a few times since they had unloaded their gear in Guam, but there was something rather sinister about him that he just couldn't figure out.

"Be careful of that one." John-Claude talked in hushed tones to Kape, hoping he wouldn't do anything stupid and get himself in trouble. Kape however, had not been happy since his basic training experience and believed in doing just enough to get by. During basic training, Kape knew that Sergeant Gopher really thought that beating the hell out of him had been enough to cure him from abdicating his duties, but Kape was too smart for that. He knew enough about human nature to know that money could get you anywhere or anything you wanted. He paid the recruits to do most of his work and the sergeant never knew it. After a while, he wasn't even afraid to miss his duties when the lower-ranking officers were around because he paid them off too. He was glad his father was a lawyer and that he too had gone into law. Daddy had connections and nothing was too good for his little boy. When Kape's father found out his son had been beaten, Sergeant Gobar had been called in early that Saturday morning. It was the Colonel's day off so Sergeant Gobar knew that it had to be pretty serious. The sergeant knocked softly on the Colonel's door.

"Come in." Sergeant Gobar removed his cap and quickly saluted the colonel.

"At ease, Sergeant. Have a seat." The colonel had been looking at some papers which were still in his hands. He looked up from his desk for the first time since Sergeant Gobar had entered.

"You are familiar with a Private Ronald Kapeheart I believe."

"Yes sir. I believe he is one of the new recruits from New York, sir."

"What in the world is going on, Sergeant? I've received some disturbing news concerning a Private Kapeheart and some unusual treatment that he received under your command. Is this true Sergeant? Colonel Bradford was a man who did not like being bothered and when his superior officer called him on his day off, it meant there was trouble. The beating of a young Private whose father was some big shot Negro lawyer up in New York had come across his desk marked 'Important and Confidential'. The colonel had come right to the point with Sergeant Gobar concerning the issue. Whenever something like this came up, the colonel knew that a favor was being called in and it was his job to make sure that it was done. The conversation was worded carefully so that Sergeant Gobar would know how to give responses without incriminating himself.

"So who was responsible for the action that took place?"

"I take full responsibility for this sir. Private Kapeheart was on guard duty and fell asleep. He also was belligerent in the mess hall and refused to eat his dinner. He received the standard disciplinary action, sir."

"And what may I ask was the standard disciplinary action Sergeant?"

"Kitchen Patrol duty, sir." The Colonel balled his fist and hit his desk with a resounding thud that let the Sergeant know he already knew exactly what happened.

"Don't lie to me Gobar! According to the medic's report, the boy had to be taken to the infirmary where he spent the night and was unable to join training activities for nearly three weeks. For God's sake man, he had broken ribs." Sergeant Gobar knew it was no use trying to conceal the incident.

"Sir. I believe that one of the officers may have gone a bit too far but I will see that it is taken care of immediately."

"See that you do, Sergeant. And by the way, make sure that Private Kapeheart is well-taken care of for the duration of his stay here. His father is one of the first Negro lawyers to ever pass the bar exam and serve as an independent attorney in Brooklyn. He's well-known and a well-respected man in his neck of the woods." The colonel dismissed Sergeant Gobar, still irritated that he had been disturbed. The Colonel's wife had promised her husband lunch would be ready for him when he returned. A woman as beautiful as she didn't have to do anything but look beautiful. He picked up the telephone to let her know he was on his way.

After the meeting with Colonel Bradford, Sergeant Gobar never told his subordinates or anyone else to give Private Kapeheart the kid glove treatment. He despised the little worm and secretly hoped he caught hell. On the contrary, he told his officers to train the group harder with grueling and rigorous exercises. It had always been an unspoken law that if a soldier had enough money, he could pay to have his is duties reassigned. The officers used the money they acquired from the 'well to do boys' to go into town on the weekends and have fun. An extra girl to party with always made an officer a lot happier.

Kape truly had the makings of a good lawyer. He was cunning yet, if you didn't know better, he was very convincing and you'd believe every word that came out of his mouth. John-Claude had no idea Kape was paying the officers off even though he knew he would give a private cash for making his bed or cleaning his gear at night while he would lay around on his bunk.

"Hey Kape! You never seem to do a damn thing around here." Private Wilson had been watching Kape for weeks. He thought it was amusing that Kape was able to get his way and it seemed that no one really cared.

"What's it to you Wilson? As long as the work gets done, right? Remember that."

During, the first month in Guam, the soldiers were assigned duties which took much of the day to complete. On weekends, the men went to the local bars. A weekend of fun carousing with the local girls and buying drinks until it was time to return to the post. A few of the relationships that began as fun turned into romantic liaisons that lasted for months. There was also the chance of diseases being passed from one to another and John-Claude was always careful whenever he ventured into town. His main reason for ever going was to be able to pen in his journal, all the things he saw. It amused him to watch how the women would advertise themselves for the soldiers who came into town. The local men always resented the soldiers and sometimes there would be brawls over the women. If the military police were called, all the soldiers would scatter to avoid disciplinary action.

Since Guam was a part of the United States, It was protected by the United States and its inhabitants. There were armed U. S. soldiers standing watch twenty four hours a day to make sure no direct contact was made with Chamarro women. There was a river that ran behind the barracks some hundred feet away. Every morning and every evening, the women would come to the river to bathe. A barbed wire fence was the only barricade between them. Some who had not been intimate with their wives or girlfriends for quite a while would get to their bunk beds, find a peep hole and watch. The men were warned however, that any attempt to physically violate the rights of these female citizens could result in death as they would be fired upon. The men, tempted by the women would make crude remarks whenever they could. John-Claude thought about women sometimes but in a different way. He couldn't fathom the possibility of impregnating a woman and then leaving her behind to raise the child alone. When the war was over, he planned to go back home and continue teaching. Women could wait.

26

In August of 1939, Hitler and Stalin aligned military forces to overthrow Poland and did so on September 1, 1939. Days later, allies for Great Britain and France vowed to support Poland which was the impetus for World War II. Between the two leaders the Baltic States of Estonia, Latvia, and Lithuania were crushed. Stalin's forces defeated Finland while the German navies sank over one hundred merchant shipping vessels bound for Britain. Norway, Denmark, Belgium and the Netherland all fell to Germany.

In the mid 1940's, Italy's dictator Mussolini, formed an alliance with Hitler and declared war against France and Britain. France signed a truce with Germany to divide the country into two zones, one under German rule and the other under French rule. The most gruesome of Hitler's atrocities was the annihilation of millions of Jews in occupied Poland but eventually Hitler's seemingly narcissistic personality ordered the takeover of the Soviet Union which was partially stalled because of dissention among Germans as well as harsh winter conditions to carry out his orders.

British Prime Minister Winston Churchill negotiated with the United States to pass the Lend-Lease Act to receive crucial aid in the onslaught of Germany warfare in Britain. Japan, with its eye on expansion, saw an opportunity to seize European colonial holdings in the Far East however, the United States, having an alliance with China, was the only country capable of standing in its way. The Japanese had negotiated oil embargoes and land from America but to no avail. As a last resort, a deadline for negotiating peace with America went unheeded. Although the United

States had broken diplomatic relation with the Japanese, retaliation was the last thing the United States expected. Japan was primarily unafraid of America and planned to strip and take control in Southeast Asia and the nearby islands. The one fear that constantly loomed in their minds was the strength of the United States Pacific Fleet, based in Pearl Harbor, Hawaii. The best strategy for defeating the fleet was to use split-second timing. Disabling this powerful base was a risky move unless they were caught off guard and the damage to their planes and navy vessels were rendered useless. The Japanese took full advantage of their surprise attack prompting the United States to enter World War II.

27

On the morning of December 7, 1941 at seven fifty-five, a Japanese warplane followed by three hundred sixty bombers bearing the country's symbol "Land of the Rising Sun" descended on Pearl Harbor, a naval base on the island of Oahu protected by the United States. As sirens blared, sailors, officers, and pilots all raced to get to positions of defense.

Using carrier planes, the Japanese raid on Pearl Harbor lasted little more than two hours. It sank battleships and destroyed many naval vessels in the process making an attack on Guam an easier target. To make matters worse, the U. S. military base in Guam was not heavily armed since it was not a major economic area but it belonged to the United States. It the Japanese were going to be malicious, the island of Guam would be a target of intimidation and a means of strong arming the United States. That night, the staff Sergeants relayed messages to the soldiers, the status of the island and how the men could best protect themselves from its possible bombing. It was very important that the soldiers were ready in case an emergency arose.

The platoon was readied and prepared for battle and protection. Each man was given basic gear, enough food to last for several days and a shovel. Just as John-Claude began to wonder why the men were given shovels, Colonel Bradford walked into the barracks and the men stood to attention. He was a well-spoken man who seemed to know exactly what he needed to say.

"Today is a very important day. Your attention to detail may very well determine whether you live or die. There's a war out there gentlemen. Everything that you have learned from your basic training will now come into play. The rumors you've heard are true. It has been confirmed that the Japanese have bombed Pearl Harbor. Within the next twenty four hours, there is a great possibility there may be an air raid on this island. Our units were called here to protect the Guamanians. There is no heavy artillery surrounding the island to hold any air attacks at bay. We are what you might call sitting ducks. If there is no fall out, then there will be no casualties. However, the only protection we have is to go underground." Being a soldier was one thing but actually being faced with the possibility of being attacked and killed by air raid bombing in the middle of nowhere was a different subject." He now had their undivided attention. As he looked in the eyes of these young soldiers, he saw the fear and fearlessness that he knew would be their strength.

"Every man is going to be the master of his fate." The sergeant commanded the soldiers to formation and as soon as everyone was ready, the men were instructed to march several feet in a varying directions. When everyone had found their designated areas, they were given further instruction.

"Each of you have been given a shovel and an area large enough for your body. Every man will dig a foxhole that is at least six feet deep. The bombs used by the Japanese are quite deadly but will not penetrate more than two feet below the ground. We will practice every morning and every evening. It will take approximately two minutes from the time you hear the siren to get into your position of shelter. Remember, whenever you hear the siren, it will mean that we are actively under attack and you will immediately retreat to your foxhole. The enemy can and will attack at any time. Make sure you find your foxhole and get into it as quickly as possible. Start digging."

John-Claude looked for Kape but did not notice him in line with the rest of the soldiers. He probably had paid someone to dig his foxhole for him. The day was nearly gone before the men finished their digging. The heat from the near one hundred fifteen degree temperatures had thoroughly baked the earth, making the soil difficult to break. John-Claude watched as some soldiers plunge their shovel into the earth as far as they could and then actually hoisted the weight of their bodies onto the shovels. It yielded the soil more quickly than the method they had been shown. He emulated the technique and was the first to finish his foxhole. Soon other soldiers used the same method to get the soil lifted more quickly. When the soldiers finished, they went to the barracks to clean up and get ready dinner. By the time John-Claude got his dinner tray and neared the table where Kape was sitting he could near him talking disparagingly about the conversation Sergeant Gobar had with the platoon earlier.

"You believe that? Do you really think the Japanese would be stupid enough to bomb this island? Just think about it. The United States would never let that happen. The fleet in Hawaii has more than enough protection to ward off any enemy. Don't believe all the talk you hear on the radio about it either. Some of these people just want a sensational story. My father told me that it technically would not be possible for this to have much impact on the world. It wouldn't even faze the U. S." John-Claude clearly understood the danger and tried to reason with him between bites food.

"But don't you think it would be a good idea to have your foxhole dug as a precautionary measure. You know that you'll get in a lot of trouble if you don't..."

"You relax and let me worry about that, Mr. Schoolteacher. Why don't you go read a book or something?" Kape laughed as he got up from the table and left the mess hall.

28

The summer and spring semesters had gone smoothly for Valery. The campus was void of most of the male students that had been there when she first arrived. Of the one hundred fifty six freshmen males that had enrolled, less than one third remained since the war effort had begun. Selective Service wrote letters, families cried, yet more men were taken to war. The young men that were left in their home states were the ones that couldn't pass the original physical examinations or the men who were lucky enough to be the only male in the a family. Valery never had time for lots of friends but the upperclassman everyone knew as Leo frequently made a point of sitting near her. She found out that Leon was never sent to war, and on one occasion, Valery had a chance to ask him why. He always spoke of one of his younger brothers so she knew he was not an only child. He told her Uncle Sam really didn't have a solid clad recruitment system. Leo's college address afforded him the luxury of not receiving his draft letter in his home state. His parents notified the draft board that he was not living there. The draft board wrote his parents back and told them to furnish them with his current address. By the time the address was furnished and the letter sent to the correct address, Leo was at home for the semester break. He took the liberty of writing the draft board to volunteer for service. The clerk made note of the information and recorded the current address. The cat and mouse scheme had worked well so far and Leo had every intention of continuing his education and becoming a great political figure in history.

The fall semester nearing its end found Valery relishing the fact that she was now an advanced sophomore and looking forward to this year. Professor Brown had written several articles that had been published of notable review by the boards of several prominent universities. In November of that same year, a letter from Dr. Carter, President of Howard University was sent inviting him to join their staff. Professor Brown was honored, although he had grown to admire his colleagues and loved his students. At first, there were mixed feelings around the campus as the news spread of his possible departure. Some of the staff would really miss him. Some would be relieved he was gone. He was a man of integrity and abhorred the prejudices that infiltrated the staff dividing light and dark skinned students. He adhered to looking at the abilities of a student void of their hue. He often wrote papers on how the inequalities of people within races would someday do more damage than racism.

One week later, after the Brown's had eaten dinner and were sitting on the front porch, President Lee came by for a visit. Recognizing the car, Professor Brown got up from his chair and stepped off the porch to meet him. Professor Lee rolled down the window extending his hand.

"I just got word that Howard University plans to extend an invitation for you to join their faculty. My sister is the President's personal secretary so she actually typed the letter. She thought she'd better let me know that I'd probably be losing you." Professor Brown wasn't sure what he should say since he had not discussed the offer with President Lee.

"Dr. Lee, I think it's an opportunity worth considering but before I make my final decision, I want to talk it over with my family. We have been here for almost ten years now, and my family has come to know this neck of the woods and the community pretty well. I particularly enjoy my work here and advising."

President Lee looked intently at Cole Brown even though he was thinking something quite different. It was reported to him that Professor Brown had recruited some dark-skinned girl named Valery Lewis from New York. The young lady was the sister of his daughter's best friend.

Her parents had been mortally wounded in a car wreck and the four year athletic scholarship would help greatly. The student was a guest in the faculty cottage with the Brown's for a while and was seen during the outrageous activities to oust his favored candidate for the election of the first dark skinned Miss Blue Keyes State. Now it was reported that she had been seen riding a bicycle around on the campus.

President Lee fully intended to have this young lady taken care of and this latest development would just make things a lot easier. If Cole Brown took another job, another staff member would be recommended to become department head. Once out of the way, President Lee would make sure the new head would be someone that was a better team player and an advocate of the traditions of Blue Keyes State. His mind drifted back as Cole asked him how his family was doing.

"Oh, very well, thank you. That grandson of mine will be turning four years old next week. His grandmother and I will be going to Chicago to visit. He has already written a Christmas list an arm long to Santa and I'm sure we'll try to fill at least half of it. You know I have to go shopping with my wife so she won't get everything on the list and leave her parents with nothing to buy for their own child. It's hard not to spoil him though. He's a good kid. Well, I really do hope that you have that talk with your wife and let me know. We value you here at Blue Keyes State College but we would never try to keep you here when you are being offered a position at a prestigious institution of learning like that of Howard." Dr. Lee had grown tired of talking to Cole and vicariously looked at his watch.

"Well, I'd stay longer but I do have an urgent meeting with the student council president in my office in about fifteen minutes." Cole Brown walked the President back to the driver side door. He got in his car and started his engine waving at Mrs. Brown as she stood at the kitchen window waiting for her husband to return.

"Good day and congratulations again. Give my regards to your wife."

"Thank you sir. I will." Cole Brown stood in the driveway as the

President drove out of sight. When he made it back inside, he stood beside his wife in silence. Aware that his silence was louder than she could ever remember she looked at her husband.

"What was that all about?" Cole Brown turned to and looked at his wife.

"I think I've just been fired."

29

John-Claude had heard the planes roar in the distant most of the day. He had no way of telling whether the planes were allies or foe although he suspected American aircraft was nearby. The soldiers had been restricted to the base for the next forty eight hours. The barracks were filled with a sense of awe as each soldier struggled within himself to remain calm yet vigilant. Some men read their Bibles. Some wrote. Some listened to music on their radios and some stared blankly into space. John-Claude took notes like a journalist of a big newspaper hoping he'd live long enough to share them. No one left the barracks that day except in emergency cases. Eating canned rations, the men sat on their bunks. They took turns going to relieve themselves hoping their last place in life wouldn't be sitting on a head. The tense emotions of the men seemed to lessen as the day went on without incident. The staff sergeant came into the barracks periodically during the day to check on the men. By night, everyone had begun to relax a bit. Perhaps there would not be a raid on Guam. The sergeants were still getting reports that a few Japanese planes could still be in the vicinity and that everyone should still be on emergency alert. He relayed the message to the soldiers. They stood at attention when Sergeant Gobar entered the room.

"At ease, men. No news does not mean good news. Message relays confirm that the Japanese may have bombers in the area. We are not out of danger. Stay alert. You are reminded again that if the siren is heard, you will have approximately two minutes to get to your foxholes. There will be no time for procrastination. Haul only your person and your weapon with you. Keep your weapon with you at all times. Understood?" A resounding 'yes sir' permeated the barracks as the soldiers seemed to realize that the man that stood before them was as important to them as their own instincts. His voice provided a kind of leadership that left them unafraid to face the enemy. It was the task before them and that night as the lights were turned off, each man made his peace and tried to sleep.

At first, John-Claude had been dreaming he was back in New York teaching history classes. He was home from the war and the students were sitting attentively in their seats listening as he reiterated the stories he had written in his journal They asked questions and he answered each and every one of them. He kept looking at this watch to be sure he ended his lecture in time to dispense homework assignments to the class. It had taken several hours to research the topics he wanted his students on which to base their term papers. He answered another question asked by one of the students. He looked at his watch once more and decided to end the session for the day. Just as he did, the bell rang. John-Claude was disappointed he would have to wait until the next class session to give the assignment. The students began to get up and leave the room. A few students came up to his desk to start a conversation with him, telling him how much they enjoyed the class. Others shook his hand and still others seemed to just talk more and more loudly. The school was performing its periodic air raid drill which meant all students were moving to the central part of the school building. John-Claude opened his eyes from the dream and sprang into action when the realization came to him that the bell he had been hearing in his dream was the siren that a bomb had been dropped above the island of Guam and was headed for them. He looked around the barracks as the lights flickered once, twice, and then out of good. He had practiced this moment a million times in his mind, but now that it had finally come, it seemed confusing. Men were moving in all directions and John-Claude knew he would need to stay calm and move quickly to his foxhole. The first bomb could be felt when it struck the small island as the men neared their foxholes. The second bomb was closer and the men could see the nearby flood of light, as if the sun had exploded, blinding their eyes painfully. Most of the men were already in their foxholes by the time John-Claude attempted to jump in his. Looking in his foxhole, he saw the face of his friend Kape peering up at him. He was scared yet it made the situation no better.

"I'm sorry man." John-Claude's instincts told him to pull him out but Kape was taller and stouter than he. It would have been impossible to do so anyway knowing the next bomb could strike the ground where he was standing in a matter of seconds.

"Get out of my foxhole Kape!"

"I can't. I didn't dig one." The only thing John-Claude could do was jump on top of Kape's body and pray. As the bomb hit the ground, he felt shrapnel searing into his face and then sharp-like needles entering his forehead causing him so much pain that he grabbed his face. That was the last thing John-Claude remembered.

30

Cole Brown had been busy working since seven o'clock with student schedules and advising them of their options. He had thought a lot about how the move from Blue Keyes State to Howard was going to affect Valery. He hoped she would continue to matriculate well. He had already advised her to work hard and to ask questions of her instructors whenever she wasn't sure of something. He even suggested she wait until after class to talk to a professor if necessary. It was good advice because on one occasion she had done so. But what Professor Brown did not realize was how much she inwardly had come to depend on the Brown family for strength and support.

Professor Bobbie Clark was the head of the physical education department. The class he taught was a requirement that every student had to take and pass in order to graduate if they were physical education majors. He was a difficult professor and often gave test questions that asked for such exactness that it was virtually impossible to pass. If you answered the question incorrectly, you received a minus two. If you didn't answer the question at all, you received a zero. If you answered the question correctly, you received a score of plus one. It was possible to receive a score of minus fifty eight points for a test grade in his class. Valery's first test grade was a minus thirteen. She had done well in all of her other classes and the test wasn't fair. The test asked for answers beyond the information that was contained in the required textbook that was in his syllabus. When the class was over that day, Valery asked

Dr. Clark about several of the test questions. He told her any good student wanting to become a physical education major should want to know more than was asked of them. He began to ask her lots of other questions although none of them pertained to the subject. After getting nowhere with him, Valery, completely exasperated, left his classroom and headed for Dr. Brown's office. After listening to Valery's side of the story Cole Brown made an appointment and met with Dr. Clark in his office about the incident. Bobbie Clark made no attempt to hide his annoyance at being called into question and got right to the point.

"What's your interest in this matter, Brown?" Cole Brown could tell that his below-the-belt comment was meant to deter his interrogation.

"I can assure you it isn't personal Dr. Clark. I just want to make sure proper protocol is being followed. One of your students, Miss Valery Lewis, came to see me to discuss a problem she's having in your class. She mentioned your grading system was difficult to follow based on the syllabus she was given at the beginning of the semester." Dr. Clark was ready to defend himself.

"My grading system is no different than school policy. However, it is my decision to create and administer quizzes based on the knowledge that all physical education majors need to know. If Miss Lewis is not capable of understanding the text...

"I'm glad you mentioned the word "text" Dr. Clark. I examined one of your quizzes and discovered it was not based on the information included in your required textbook. I have looked at the grading of several of your quizzes and noted the grades are given arbitrarily. Receiving minus zero grades are not prescribed in your syllabus nor the college student hand book. One last thing. I am very much aware that your quizzes are being graded by your student assistants." Professor Brown uncharacteristically lowered his voice and leaned in toward Bobbie Clark's chair.

"Just know that if any more allegations come across my desk, I will take you before the college disciplinary committee." Dr. Cole stood up and left his office. He hoped Dr. Clark would heed the warning. Bobbie Clark was incensed that Valery Lewis had the audacity to report him to Cole Brown. Just who did she think she was? He made a mental note of it. Then he picked up the telephone in his office.

31

Bobbie Clark was a native Virginian whose background was meager at best. He had been poor most of his life yet he struggled to rise through his athletic prowess to a college graduate, was named assistant coach at Blue Keyes State, for a few years was promoted to head of the physical education department. Not knowing who his father was, he was raised by his mother Lorena. She, being a domestic worker with no formal education, worked from sun up to sun down to please her employers. Her humbleness landed her in bed with most of them. She couldn't complain for fear of losing her job and cutting off the only support she had for herself and little Bobbie. She and her son lived in an area known as 'The Bottom', where the main activity in the small town was the night life. Lorena was eventually lured to the night clubs as men would see her coming to and from work. Bobbie followed his mother around even as a young boy since she had no relatives who would keep an eye on him while she worked. He grew up seeing much of his mother's activities and although he hated the men he realized he could capitalize on their good fortune.

Bobbie Clark began to know the men in his mother's life. They were mostly professional men and coal mining executives who were married and just looking for an outlet from their boring housewives. Bobbie kept their dirty little secrets in exchange for personal favors to him. His first job after his college graduation as high school football coach was virtually handed to him even though there were others that were more experienced for the position than he. It had been as easy as waiting outside the doorstep of their one bedroom house. Bobbie knew the man inside with his mother was an administrator for the Virginia School system. Being a well-known and respected administrator in the community made the request even sweeter. He had known many other of his mom's suitors with whom he had become familiar and with whom verbal contracts were made. His connections had landed him the job of his dreams at Blue Keyes and he intended to enjoy it.

It was a known a fact that Professor Clark enjoyed the prestige that was connected to being a college professor, and especially when it involved young, pretty girls. Valery Lewis didn't fit in his picture as a memorable face and giving her a less than deserving grade was of no consequence to him. If she wanted a better grade, she could work for it like all the others. It amused him to watch the naïve freshmen and sophomores stand outside his door waiting for him to come out, trying to strike up conversations with him. He thought that Valery was probably just like one of them. He didn't like the dark ones though. He had always been partial to the fair-skinned women. So was President Lee. Bobbie and he were in the same fraternity and the incoming freshmen that year had irked even the alumni chapter when they decided to revolt against their choice for Miss Blue Keyes Homecoming Queen. They needed to be taught a lesson. There would always be a place for darker-skinned students, but as far as he was concerned, they would always undergird those whose hues were more commensurate with their fair-skinned or white counterparts. Professors like Cole Brown were advocates of all students and particularly concerned with the treatment of the darker skinned ones.

Valery didn't know what Professor Brown had said or done on her behalf but she was certainly glad that her final grade for the semester was one she deserved. Valery walked up to the second floor administration building. Professor Brown was in his office with the door open.

"Come in Valery. I'm glad you came by. How are things with you?"

"Great! Just thought I'd drop by and say hello."

"I'm glad you did. I have some news to tell you." Valery had hoped that the news would be a promotion for him to an even higher position or that perhaps Mrs. Brown was pregnant. Or that the sky was falling in. Anything except the words that rolled off his tongue.

"You're what?" Valery didn't mean to show so much expression. After all, he wasn't her father. He was someone that she had come to know as a friend. But how could he just leave her behind? Why had he not mentioned it to her before now? It was as if he could hear every word aloud that she had thought silently.

"Yes, Valery. I was offered a position to teach at Howard University. The department head told me that he had been reading the articles that I had published in the Negro Gazette. They were impressed with the research and have offered me nearly twice the salary I make here." Valery could feel the tears as they began to well in her eyes. How could she be happy about what she was hearing and at the same time not be? He got up from his desk and walked over to her. He could tell she was trying very hard to control her emotions.

"Don't you see? This is a once in a lifetime offer. Howard is one of the best schools in the country. They have an excellent faculty. The salary increase will be substantial and I can finally start thinking about building a real home for my family. There are so many things that I have wanted to do for quite a while that moving to this position will enable me to do." Valery realized how her face must have looked and she quickly tried to smile and congratulate him.

"I'm sorry. I just wasn't expecting that. I am so happy for you. You really deserve it. When are you leaving? Cole had thought about it.

"I think we'll stay here until the end of next semester. That will give me a chance to tie up all the loose ends here and I will join Howard's staff in the fall." Valery stayed and talked to Dr. Brown for a while longer. When she got up to leave, he hugged her although he could imagine how she must really have felt inside. He assured her that he and his wife would keep in touch with her through calls and letter writing to make sure things were going well.

The semester moved along quickly with Valery making mostly A's and B's in all of her classes. She had carried eighteen hours and was hoping to carry twenty one hours in the spring. She began to think more often what life at Blue Keyes would be like without the Browns. They would be moving in two weeks and though she hated to see them leave, they deserved a chance to move up in the world. Valery knew that a few of the faculty members were probably jealous of the fact that Dr. Brown was invited to join the prestigious staff of Howard University. It didn't happen often but it couldn't have happened to a finer man. Jolene and Mary came down from New York to help the family move. Mary knew that without Jolene's transportation, it might be a while before she would see her sister again. The morning of the Brown's departure from Blue Keyes, Valery saw a note under her door. She picked it up. It read:

To Whom It May Concern,

> As of May 15, 1943, all bicycles owned by students enrolled at Blue Keyes State College are prohibited on campus. Only vehicles with permits will be allowed on the campus grounds. All other modes of transportation are in violation of Blue Keyes State College Handbook Code 587 pertaining to motor vehicle safety. All students found in violation of this law will be fined could face indefinite suspension or expulsion.

> President Samuel Lee

When Valery read the letter, it angered her. The bicycle was kept in her room. She rode it to and from class and on occasions when her physical education classes had stretched her muscles too tightly. No one had ever complained about it before. Why now? She wished she had someone to talk to about it. But Valery didn't have a roommate during her sophomore year due to some mix up with campus housing. Charlene had been the only person she'd enjoyed as a roommate but having extra privacy and quiet was okay too. She took her bath and got dressed realizing that there was really nothing she could do about the new rule. Twenty minutes later there was a knock on her door. She swung the door open to see her sister and Jolene standing there. Valery screamed and grabbed them both, pulling them inside her room. She was so happy to see her sister again. They would now have to save up for bus and cab fare to visit each other and get around in the city. The three talked for a while and Valery showed them the letter she had received under her door. Mary read it and passed it to Jolene. Mary was the first to comment.

"Can you believe it? Bikes are so common in New York. Everybody rides them. I'm sure that we can take this matter up with someone." Jolene knew from her father's experiences that Blue Keyes State College was steeped in traditions and would not easily change. There was no chance the decision would be overturned, especially since it had been signed by the president. Jolene, like her father, thought that a more passive approach would be better than confronting the administration.

"I suggest that you dispose of the bicycle for now. Keep your eyes open for anyone you see riding a bicycle. If you do, find the owner and ask them if there are any rules about bicycles on campus. Chances are, if the bike belongs to someone that is in the President's corner, nothing will be done. Then you may ride yours and if you receive a second warning letter, you will have the proof you need to take action. Daddy always says that fighting fire with fire doesn't always work. Sometimes you get more bees with honey. Anyway, we're not going to spoil our day over a silly bicycle, are we? We came here to see you kiddo." Valery laughed and pretended to forgot about the bicycle incident. Deep down, with the Browns leaving, that bicycle would have given her a way to assuage the loss of what would feel like her parents dying all over again.

Mae Belle Brown waited at the cottage for the girls to return and after a mid- morning snack consisting of cold-cut sandwiches, chips, and colas, they drove to town searching for larger empty boxes that store owners had placed outside their businesses. Mrs. Brown purchased several rolls of packing tape to seal the boxes and picked up old newspapers from wives of some of the faculty members who were eager to help. Whenever Valery didn't have a class, she had been riding her bicycle down to the Brown's helping them pack and box up eight years of accumulation that would soon vacate Blue Keyes State and move to Howard University. A week later, the Brown's had a large moving van pull up to the cottage and load nearly all their belongings. Jolene's trunk was full and Valery had ridden her bicycle down the campus for the last time just for kicks before she put it in the trunk of the car. Hugs, kisses, and tears all mingled together as the moving van rolled slowly down the graveled driveway with the Brown's, Jolene, and Mary right behind it. Valery would never forget the Brown's and they would never forget her.

32

John-Claude's upper body lay lifeless after the bomb had hit. Kape, trapped beneath him stayed quiet for as long as he could. He could hear the sounds of orders being bellowed, the medics sounding their horns and the soldiers climbed out of nearby foxholes calling the names of their comrades. John-Claude's body was beginning to feel heavier and Kape was sure that he must have taken a direct hit. He called his name several times but John-Claude did not respond. The thought of him standing underneath a dead man made him sick and he began screaming hysterically. John-Claude was pulled from the foxhole. His body was limp and by the time the medics got to him, his face was covered with blood. Kape scrambled from the foxhole and desperately called out to him. He was ashamed of what he had done and moreover, afraid that it might have cost his friend's life.

"John-Claude." Kape called even more loudly until the medic demanded that he move back. With little light to see, the medic thought that John-Claude would end up being another casualty, but after looking more closely, he detected movement from his body. As he wiped some of the blood away, he could see the soldier's facial features were still intact but a considerable amount of shrapnel was stuck in his forehead. The shrapnel needed to be removed. Luckily he was not in mortal danger. The medics left him there and went on to more serious cases. When John-Claude came to, he was laying on the ground. There was a man standing over him explaining he had been struck by debris from a bomb. He was told that there were pieces of metal in his forehead that would have to be removed. He was indeed very lucky not to have been killed. Anesthesia was at a premium and would only be used in the most serious of cases. He would have the shrapnel removed without any painkilling medicine.

"Do you drink soldier?"

"No, sir." John-Claude groaned at the searing pain he felt all over his face.

"Good. Drink this." Before John-Claude could resist, a liquid was being forced down his throat. It was so strong, it took his breath away and turned his head.

"You'd better drink some more of this son. This is going to hurt like hell." He began to feel warm inside and took another long swallow of the foul tasting liquid given him. John-Claude heard another voice.

"Squeeze my hand soldier." The medic had what looked to John-Claude like a giant pair of tweezers.

"Here we go." The medic pulled out one of the larger pieces of shrapnel. It felt like a piece of his skin had been ripped brutally from his head. He tried not to scream but he had never felt that much pain in his life. As the second piece was being removed, he passed out and when he awoke, he was in the infirmary. Feeling groggy, he reached up and felt for his forehead. As his hand moved across his face, he could feel a thick cloth-like material had been wrapped around his head. At first, his thoughts were hazy, but he slowly began to remember the sequence of events that had happened. Where was he or how long had he been there? He wasn't really sure. He remembered the dream that woke him up. He remembered running to his foxhole and seeing Kape cowering down inside and then a very loud blast. The doctor, who had been making this rounds from soldier to soldier, peered down at him, and began asking him questions about the accident. It had been assumed that John-Claude had not made it to his foxhole in time being the reason he was injured from the bomb blast. He knew that was not the truth but he hesitated to say more. Reporting Kape would not help his condition and if Kape had not jumped in, he could have been killed. Later, rumors circulated among the soldiers that Kape had deliberately planned to jump in John-Claude's foxhole if a threat was eminent. The soldiers thought Kape's actions were deplorable and intended to do something about it. It was extremely rare for soldiers to share information to officers but Kape had it coming. Many of the soldiers had worked with John-Claude, saw him dig his foxhole, and knew he didn't deserve to have been injured in the bombing. They felt that nobody deserved to endure that type of punishment simply because another soldier was too lazy to provide protection for his own life. Private Ronnie Kapeheart was summoned by his superior officers and an investigation proved that he never dug his foxhole. His actions were in direct violation of a superior officer. His sentence was deliberate and swift. Kape was given a dishonorable discharge from the military. Now his career as a lawyer would probably never materialize.

John-Claude, while in the hospital, spent his time writing in his journal for several weeks before he was able to return to active duty. When he did return to duty, he noticed he wasn't able to hear as well as he had before the accident and it affected his judgement. After further evaluations, he was given a medical discharge. John-Claude left Guam and returned to the states. He signed up and was placed in the ASTP unit, a unit consisting of all Negro soldiers who were at the top of their class and would be paid accordingly. John-Claude was sorry that the bomb had injured him but he was one of the lucky ones. During the bombing in Guam, there had been more than one thousand casualties including women and children. But war was over for John-Claude, at least for now. Bringing all his memories with him, he left the war-torn island of Guam and was flown to Hawaii for two weeks, after which time he returned to New York. While in Hawaii, he listened to radio coverage of the devastation brought by the war. He still couldn't help but wonder why world leaders could not resolve their differences of opinion. In later years, John-Claude learned that President Roosevelt had been sent a warning about the bombings that were to take place in the Hawaiian Island, but due to delays in its transmission, it arrived too late. Putting the past behind, John-Claude felt like a free man and he could only look to his future.

33

It had been warm in the Hawaiian Islands and John-Claude had enjoyed his two week stay. Going home meant greeting the brisk New York winds. He would only have two weeks there to visit with his family before his reassignment to the Army Standard Training Program. His mother was giddy with excitement to see her son. He had picked up small gifts everywhere he'd gone. He gave his mother a beautiful apron with the map of the Pacific Ocean on it. It showed both the Hawaiian and Guam Island on it. She adored it because it was all she prayed about when she knew that was where he was going. She had strong faith in God and believed He would not let anything happen to her son. He gave his brother a sheathed knife. It was a particular brand that only army personnel could acquire. The sheath was made of pure leather and worth quite a bit of money in the states. His brother was now a senior in high school and had plans of volunteering for the military when he finished. John-Claude knew that if he could talk his brother out of going he would but if he really wanted to go he could do nothing to stop him. He couldn't deny that he had learned more about life in the year that he had been there, than he had in nearly all of his life.

John-Claude's two weeks were spent close to home, enjoying being with his family. His mother cooked all his favorite meals and he couldn't believe how wonderful it felt being there. His room looked just as it had when he left. He got out the family photo albums and looked at all the life he had lived realizing how precious it had been. He was indeed blessed to be a part of such a loving household. Some of the faculty from the school where he had taught heard he was at home and dropped by to see him. They all wanted to know if he would be coming back to teach after the winter holiday season was over. They asked him if he would be attending church on Sunday to which he affirmed and he did attend church that very Sunday. The congregation gave his a standing ovation as he was ushered to the front. His mother beamed with price as he stood stately in his army dress uniform. His students cheered his name over and over and he felt embarrassed but he stood there just the same. That Sunday, Pastor Elijah preached about the benefits of giving. He shared with his congregation that money was the lowest form of prosperity. They all laughed and nodded their heads when he asked them what all the money in the world would do for them if they were as sick as a mule. The children sang beautiful renditions of traditional songs that talked about love and giving. It was the holiday season and the sense of sharing was in the air. Once during the service, John-Claude reached up and brushed away a tear. At the end of the service, the Pastor Jay and many members came to pay their respects to him with hugs, handshakes with soft money shares, and kisses from the elderly members of the church.

"Thank you Brother Adams for coming back to see us. We've missed you so much and you've been in our prayers. Please let us know if there is anything we can do for you. Your mother has kept us informed about your injury. God spared your life for a reason and you are an inspiration to our young men. God bless you, my son.

"Thank you Pastor Elijah. God be with you also. Please keep me in your prayers." The two men shook hands vigorously. Then his mother, flanked by John-Claude and his brother left the church for home.

The next day, John-Claude received parcel from the United States Army Division. It informed him that the ASTP training that had originally been scheduled to begin at Fort Story in Virginia Beach was being rescheduled to take place at Blue Keyes State College, in Blue Keyes, West Virginia.

The military had an important rubber plant there and the presence of the military would serve as protection for the plant should an enemy attempt infiltration. Since Germany and Italy had also declared war against the United States, all major plants and industries could possibly be targets. The men would train for a one year period after which, they would be allowed to return to active duty as an officer with significant rank or continue additional training to become a ranked officer in the ASTP program. John-Claude was proud that he would be given another chance to serve the army in a different capacity. He wanted to make a difference.

His time in New York went by quickly and John-Claude spent time visiting schools and sharing his military experiences to students who would soon be part of the Selected Service Draft Program. When it was finally time to leave, he mulled over his bedroom making sure to arrange every neatly. At exactly six o'clock the next morning, there was a knock on the front door. He loaded his bags in the trunk of the army recruiter's car. He kissed his mother's forehead and stepped back to look at her one last time.

"I love you mother. Be sure to take good care of yourself." He shook his brother's hands and quickly stepped into the front seat of the car. He hated leaving but he felt happier this time because he knew he'd be going to a safer place. He was looking forward to seeing the campus of Blue Keyes State College. He never forgot about the young girl named Valery he had met on his way to Fort Story and wondered if she was still there. There would be about 150 recruits going to Blue Keyes. The men would be traveling on the Pow Tan Arrow, the train used to carry military personnel and the larger than life equipment for training that would eventually be transported to the college.

34

President Lee had been notified in October that the Federal Government would need portions of the Blue Keyes State College facility in January to house and train Negro soldiers. The college would be financially rewarded for such accommodations to which the president was pleased. He had numerous meetings with the heads of different committees on campus and was awaiting word from the board although he didn't need their approval. As a matter of common courtesy however, he met ceremoniously with them. It always gave him a sense of hierarchy to sit at the head of the table in the conference room and look down at his constituents. Being the president of a college had always been his dream and he would do anything to make sure the control of power stayed within his grasp for as long as possible. Every newspaper in town would come to the campus to interview him and to see the ASTP soldiers. The locals would spread the story and more students would be enticed to enroll. As President Lee saw it, as the enrollment increased, so would tuition and pretty soon Blue Keyes State College would be a household word. He wanted to be there to take his bow. No one would ever deprive him of that honor.

Now that the Browns were gone, Valery was virtually without friends. She spent as little time as possible talking to other students. She only had a year and a summer left at Blue Keyes. Each semester, she had taken more hours than were required and still maintained an overall rating of above proficiency. Her 3.65 grade point average did not award her the dean's list status, but it did mean that she was in good standing with the college and would be in a position to graduate earlier than most students who started out with her. Professor Brown had been instrumental in making sure that she pushed herself to take maximum hours while providing tutors for her before he left for Howard University.

Since many of the men had been drafted into the service, one of the male dorms was vacated and given to the females. Although most of the girls declined to move. Valery was happy to do so since it meant, once again, she would be without a roommate. She opted for a room on the first floor. She was lucky to have run into Charlene on her way from lunch accompanied by two other girls that Valery didn't know.

"What a-r-e going on?" Charlene was a big kidder. Being an English major entitled her use of the common slang. They both hugged each other and laughed.

"It's been a while since we've seen each other. We'll, allow me to introduce my friend Denise from Beckley, West Virginia and this is my roommate Pamela from Columbus, Ohio. This is Valery Lewis, my former roommate. All three girls exchanged pleasant greetings.

"I heard you were on the list of students moving to Welch Hall. Is it really true? Charlene was just kidding around but Valery thought she'd play along with her.

"Yeah. I thought if I got away from you crazy girls in Waters Hall, I could get some sleep at night. By the way, if you three are not too busy, I could surely use a hand in moving. The girls didn't mind helping Valery since their classes would be over in a few hours. They discussed the upcoming dance that would be held the next night. It was square-dancing night and although Valery didn't do much dancing, she did enjoy seeing the students listen to the calls and watching the couples execute the procedures. She had already decided to wear her long black skirt and white blouse. Mary had given her a full petticoat to wear under it but it made her feel silly so she didn't wear it. She preferred being more ordinary.

She stuck to her goals of graduating and helping Mary get back to NYU. Valery had made that secret promise to herself after her mother and father died. She felt they were looking down from heaven and she would not disappoint them.

"Valery…did you hear me? I asked if you'll be joining us tonight at the dance." "Yes, I will be there. I'll owe you three for your help.

35

The train arrived in Blue Keyes around one o'clock that morning. It had taken 14 hours to get there by train. The accommodations on the train made John-Claude feel as if he was living in a palace in comparison to the experience he'd had in Guam. The porter had spent extra time helping the soldiers put their luggage in the storage compartments. The storage rooms on the train were full to capacity. He had boarded the train at 11:30 the previous morning and had slept for more than 10 hours. He ate no food that night and no breakfast the next morning. He was awakened from his sleep by the smells coming from the dining hall. The tables were full of ham and turkey sandwiches, potato salad and frosted colas. Most of the soldiers slept after the meal but John-Claude took out his pad and wrote of the spectacular view. Looking at the scenery from the train reminded him of a Christmas fairy tale. He could imaging seeing children frolicking in the snow, making snowmen, sledding down the steep hills, and rolling in thick blankets of foam-like snow. Before John-Claude realized it, hours had passed. Many of the soldiers who had been sleeping were beginning to awaken. They went to the onboard lavatory to freshen up and all found their places at the dining table. The porters noticed that everyone waited for John-Claude to bless the food before they ate. As heads bowed, the only sounds that could be heard were the clacking train wheels on the track.

"Dear Father, we thank you for the food we are about to receive for the nourishment of our bodies. Forgive us for our sins forever. Amen." The men repeated "amen' and the meal commenced. The soldiers reminisced about the politics of war. Some had seen a lot of bloodshed. Others were slightly wounded or had witnessed others being hurt by enemy fire. It seemed an awful thing to talk about during a meal but somehow talking about it eased the grievance the men felt for having taken part in a war that caused much death and destruction. Sometimes they told funny stories too. The evening went well and prior to everyone going to sleep John-Claude encouraged the men to sing songs. So they sang songs about the war, about love and about God. They arm wrestled, played cards, and even showed each other the dances that were popular in their home towns. It was an evening to remember.

Most of the soldiers slept after the meal but John-Claude took out his pad and wrote of the spectacular view. Looking at the scenery from the train reminded him of a Christmas fairy tale. He could imaging seeing children frolicking in the snow, making snowmen, sledding down the steep hills, and rolling in thick blankets of foam-like snow. Before John-Claude realized it, hours had passed.

At one o'clock the next morning, the Powtan Arrow rolled into sleepy Blue Keyes, West Virginia. Porters helped the men get all of their luggage and equipment from the train cars. It took nearly three hours to unload and reload the buses and military trucks that were awaiting their arrival. The sergeant in command gave instructions to the soldiers.

"Good morning. I know that you all are anxious to get in warm vehicles and get to your destination. However, I want to make clear our expectation of your conduct. Your housing will take place on the campus of Blue Keyes State College. This campus is currently being utilized by students, mostly females." You could see nodding heads and hear soldiers murmuring in approval.

"Attention!!"

"Yes sir!!" Their stance immediately returned to that of disciplined soldiers.

"Be it known that the President of this college is responsible for the well-being of every student that has enrolled for matriculation. You will conduct yourselves as has been stated in the military guidelines. If you break any of the stated guidelines you will be expelled from the ASTP program and possibly face a dishonorable discharge. Are we clear?

"Yes sir!!" President Lee had stipulated that the military division was to arrive on the campus between the hours of three and five o'clock that morning. He did not want to disturb the campus any more than was necessary. At the same time however, the President knew that marching one hundred fifty men on a college campus at that time of morning would arouse even more of a stir which was exactly what he wanted to happen.

As the trucks rolled on campus, there were faces pressed against the windows peering out as if something had descended from heaven. The lights in the dorms had long been out, but with the war going on, no one could be too careful. The doors in the hallways began to open as students began tapping on each other's doors inquired about the sound of trucks entering the campus at such an hour. The next morning, a paper had been placed under the doors of every student on the campus. The letter read:

Dear Students,

> In accordance with the United States Government, it has become necessary for our college to be utilized as a military training facility. Blue Keyes State College was chosen because of its fine reputation for educational excellence. The 150 men that will be training here are fine examples of our U. S. military. All students are expected to adhere to the college handbook rules of conduct. Any student that fails to comply will be expelled immediately. There will be an assembly in the gym at 9:30 a.m. for further instructions.

> President Samuel Lee

Doors began to open more quickly than usual that day. The girls whispered in soft tones of seeing military trucks roll past their dorms and what it could possibly mean. The excitement was building with the realization that if more men were on campus, they would no longer have to throw themselves at the mercy of the existing male population for dates to social activities. There would be even more reasons now to dress up and wear makeup. Everyone was hoping the men would show up at breakfast. They weren't disappointed. It took an extra thirty minutes to get them all seated in the dining hall. They were dressed in military uniform and so regimented that attention was paid to little else. Valery seated herself at her usual table and watched as the extra men filled the dining hall. The men had been signaled to stand by their military leadership and did so until the grace had been sung. They did not participate in singing but their girth dictated the utmost respect that could be given. Several girls looked at each other and giggled. Some pretended not to notice and others deliberately invited themselves to the men with their eyes. The men sat alongside the students but had no conversations with them. Valery simply watched and wondered if she would lose her room and have to move again since the additional men might need the space. She didn't have much of an appetite and after a few bites of food, she dismissed herself from the table. She had a slight headache and decided to go back to her room.

The morning air was brisk but the sky was so clear that it hurt her eyes to look at it. Valery loved looking at the winter snow even as it began to melt around the campus. The trees had a bit of white left on them that reminded her a giant ice cream cone. As she rounded the corner to the top of the incline, she thought someone called her name. She didn't stop until she distinctly heard her name called a bit more loudly and she turned around.

"Is your name Valery Lewis?" Her eyes stared into the face of a young man dressed in uniform.

"Yes. I am Valery Lewis. And who may I ask are you?" Valery thought that he must have asked someone at the table what her name was and hoped to use it as a way to start up a meaningless conversation. She really didn't appreciate the 'come on' but decided that she would be quite a lady about it.

"Well, well, well. It's been two years, and yet, I've found you! Valery could feel her rising resentment along with her headache mounting. She had heard just about enough and decided to end it.

"Is there some point to this conversation, if not, I really have important things to do." John-Claude was becoming amused with her tart responses but didn't want to upset her.

"You really don't remember me, do you?"

"Am I supposed to remember you from somewhere?" John-Claude refreshed her memory.

"Two years ago, you and I rode on a Greyhound bus that left New York heading south. You were coming to this college and I was going to Fort Story, Virginia. Does that ring a bell?" Valery began to walk back toward him. When they were within arm's reach, she looked intently in his eyes.

"You couldn't be….. John-Claude? It is you! I mean …uh…how are you? I didn't recognize you!" Valery could feel the blood rushing to her face even though the wind made her cheeks tingle. He had gained a little weight and somehow his face looked somewhat different. She surmised he must have been injured because his face had been scarred but he was the same handsome John-Claude that sat and talked with her on that bus two years ago. All of a sudden she felt terribly awkward and ill at ease. She didn't know what to say.

During the time of their separation, Valery Lewis had crossed John-Claude's mind more times than he would like to have admitted. Now that she was standing face to face, he too, was at a loss for words. After what seemed like an eternity went by, John-Claude spoke.

"It's good to see you." He extended his hand toward her. Valery responded in like kind. When their two hands met, he immediately turned his hand upward, leaving hers on top. To emphasize their reunion, he gently placed his free hand on top of hers and pressed them together.

"I'll see you later. We have a lot of catching up to do." John-Claude turned quickly and began to walk briskly back to the dining hall.

Valery half walked and half floated to the dorm. When she got to her room and opened the door, one of the students who had walked past her while she was talking to John-Claude was the first to make a cutting remark.

"Well…it didn't seem to take you long to jump one of the soldiers boys, sweetie. And we all thought you were Miss Goody Two Shoes. You really had us all fooled." Valery turned and faced the girl who had spoken to her. She closed the door without saying anything since she felt that the comment was unworthy of an answer. She still couldn't believe that she had seen him. It had been two years and her thoughts of whether he had made it back home had always haunted her and to think he was now right here on the campus! She had always thought when the time was right she would find the right man for her. Perhaps the time had come.

36

The gymnasium was much closer to full capacity with the addition of the hundred fifty military men that had arrived. At exactly nine o'clock that morning, President Lee, who had been sitting behind the podium, stood. The student body immediately ceased all conversations and turned their attention to him. On the stage with him was the Vice President of Student Affairs, the President of the Board of Directors, several white men dressed in military attire, and Student Government President Steven Cook who had earned the title 'Stool Pigeon'. They postured very piously and Valery thought they all looked like little wind-up toys. The President began with his usual welcome and commended the student body on their fine conduct and the way in which their pride illuminated every aspect of the campus. He asked the Chaplain to come forward and give the invocation after which he began his oration of the events that led to the bombing of Pearl Harbor.

Valery listened intently as President Lee explained who the soldiers were and why they were on the campus. He boasted of the impressive grade point averages that the men had obtained to be eligible for inclusion into the ASTP program. He was really proud to say once again that Blue Keyes State College was chosen above all other colleges. The other military men that shared the stage with the President were introduced and gave brief comments. Many wondered how long the men would be on the campus but the question was answered when the Major who was now at the podium cited their year-long training sessions. At first, Valery who had been trying to discreetly look for John-Claude in the crowd, was happy to hear he would be there at least a year. John-Claude too, had tried to watch for Valery that morning and when the assembly was dismissed, he stationed himself at the bottom of the stairway so that he would hopefully see her as the students filed out. At last, Valery appeared at the doorway and John-Claude made his way through the crowd so that she could see him. She waved and made her way to his side. This time, it was she who spoke first.

"I didn't know if I would see you anymore until lunch or dinner. I usually have an eight o'clock class on Mondays but since we had the assembly this morning, it was cancelled but my next class will be starting in a little while. You know, I really don't get a chance to do much socializing. She hoped he would say something soon since she couldn't seem to think of anything else to say.

"I know what you mean," he said evenly. We've been given a schedule and I think that most of the day will be spent on familiarizing ourselves with the location. I'm not at liberty to discuss any details with you but you really know as much as I do for the moment. We're here to be trained for the military so…" His voice trailed off as the other men who were leaving the gym lined in formation. John-Claude moved away from Valery and mouthed, 'see you later'. She smiled and began to walking briskly to her class. She knew she could never be late for her classes. It was hard enough having dark-skin. She had no intention of antagonizing the professional bigots any more than necessary. It had been different when Professor Brown was there. He had spoken up for her kind. But he wasn't there now so she had to be careful to not only make good grades on her assignments but to also go the extra mile just to make sure her grades did not slip.

37

Valery ran up the stairs and was one of the first ones to arrive in Anatomy 301. She liked to sit in the front of the classroom. It always gave her a sense of focus. The semester had just begun and Valery was glad she had decided to come as soon as she had. By the time the bell rang for class to begin, there were no available seats left. Professor James, who was traditionally a by-the-book man, walked into the room, greeted the students and began calling the roll. When he finished, the door opened and Juanita Johns, one of the seniors who had run for Miss Blue Keyes State College walked in, turning heads. She looked around the room for a place to sit but there were no seats left. It was obvious that she was late and Valery felt sorry for her. She had no choice but to leave.

"I'm sorry Miss. This class is full. I believe that I'm teaching this same class on Tuesdays and Thursdays in the afternoon. You will have to get your schedule changed."

"Oh please, Professor James. I have to take this class to graduate. It's my last chance. I having to take all of my coursework this spring and if I don't take it now, I won't be able to graduate." The Professor looked up from his roll book and as the young lady came up to the front of the room, she stared at him with the most beautiful eyes that even Valery had ever seen. Juanita had a light brown complexion with below the shoulder length hair that was full of body that every way she turned her head, it fell like waves cascading across an ocean. The Professor cleared his throat hard at first. His reply almost sounding apologetic.

"That's no problem. Simply have the counselor to change your schedule to take the class in the evening." Juanita was used to having her way and saw no reason why today should be any different. She wanted to take the class in the morning because her evenings were always filled with dates. She enjoyed having her pick of the men on campus. That was before the new soldiers arrived. She knew if she sulked just a little more, he would give in. Her best friend had bet her a ride into town and a ticket to the movies if she pulled it off. She was half way there.

"My evening classes are required too, Professor James, and they won't be offered again. If I change my schedule at all, it will mean I won't be able to graduate. Please help me Professor James." The Professor glanced at Miss Johns from head to toe and felt that he had to do something to help her.

"Is there anyone who would be willing to take this class in the evening?" There was silence throughout the room.

"Anyone?" He looked around hoping that someone would come forward. After it became unquestionably clear that no one was going to volunteer to leave, Professor James picked up his roll book and scanned the names with his index finger. It must have been the fate of the gods for him to stop where he did.

"Valery Lewis." Valery knew what was coming and she thought she was well prepared for it.

"Yes, Professor James?"

"Would you be so kind as to reschedule to the evening class, dear?"

"But I've already bought my book for the class and it's a requirement for me too." It was the only thing Valery could think of in defense of staying in the class. But the Professor was a step ahead of her.

"Oh, it's still no problem. Just let uh...what is your name young lady?"

"I'm Johns. Juanita Johns, sir."

"Just let Miss Johns use your book. You won't need it until tomorrow afternoon. She can go by the bookstore sometime today and get one. Right, Miss Johns?" Juanita looked at Valery and winked her eye.

"Thank you so much Professor James and thank you honey, you don't know how much this means to me."

The silence in the room was deafening as Valery slowly got up from her seat, handed Juanita her book and walk out of the room. She wanted to scream and cry but she knew it would do no good. Who would come to her rescue now? She went immediately to student affairs in the administration building to register a complaint. When she finished doing so she had her schedule changed. By the time Valery finished waiting in the long line, it was time to prepare for lunch. She had been angry, but felt better the moment she saw John-Claude smile and wave at her.

"Hello, there. How has your day been so far?" Valery smiled and lied.

"Okay, I guess. How about yours? John-Claude had had a wonderful day except for the fact that Valery kept creeping in his mind.

"I'm starving. Let's eat!" John-Claude was not in uniform wearing a pair of khaki slacks and an olive-colored shirt. The colors seemed to accentuate his fair complexion. Valery couldn't help but notice but she kept her thoughts to herself. As the two of them walked into the dining hall together, several heads turned, but the two just ignored the stares and walked ahead to the table. Once all the students were seated and served, John-Claude who intentionally sat beside Valery really talked candidly to her for the first time since their chance meeting on the Greyhound bus.

"Let me be the first to say that I really wasn't too excited about serving in the army after I came back from Guam but when I found out our unit would be training here, I remembered you told me you might be going to this college. I had hoped you'd be here and here you are." As Valery listened and watched John-Claude, she wondered about the deep scars on his forehead. She asked him to tell her more about Guam. Maybe he would tell her what happened to him. She knew there were thousands of men that had been killed or injured during the war and to know someone that had actually been there saddened but intrigued her. John-Claude wondered how much he could tell her. Should he tell her how disgustingly brutal it really was? People killing men with whom they had never quarreled. Killing them simply because governments couldn't get along. How could he tell her that his wounds were cause by the negligence of a friend? A friend who cared about no one nothing other than his own selfish whims? By the time John-Claude and Valery finished talking, most of the students had already left the dining hall. When he casually looked down at his watch, he abruptly stopped talking.

"I didn't realize it was this late. I have a briefing at thirteen hundred hours but it shouldn't last long. Would you like to get together later? I didn't give you much of a chance to talk."

"It's okay John Claude. I'd like to but I must go the library. I'm doing some research for one of my classes and I must complete it before the week is over." It was the first time she had called him by his name and it felt good. He wasn't sure if she would mind if he went along with her to the library so he asked her.

"I haven't been to the library yet. Why don't I meet you there? I promise I won't distract you in any way." Valery looked at his face more closely. There was no possibility of her saying no so they decided to meet there after dinner. She could get some of her research done while he was at his briefing. Valery stopped by the office in the dorm to pick up her mail. There were two letters for her. One was from the Brown's. The other one was from her sister. She went to her room, sat on the side of her bed and tore into the letter from the Brown's first. It read:

Dear Valery,

> Hope this letter finds you well. We are still settling in here. The weather is quite cold but the roads are not bad to travel. I spoke with the head of the Science Department here and they have a good physical education program. If you transfer here however, you will lose too many credits. Howard University will not take more than half of them.

That would cause you to have to stay in school at least another year. Otherwise, I would send for you today. Mae Belle sends her love and wants you to know that she misses you deeply. Jolene is doing fine. Write us a line or two when you get a chance. I know how busy you must be this semester.

Best Wishes,
Professor Brown

Valery thought about the wonderful times they'd had together. After they left, there were times that made her feel like packing up and joining them at Howard University but Professor Brown had been right to discourage her from wasting another year by transferring there. He and Valery had carefully mapped out her strategy to get out of school in three years instead of four. He had always known it was possible to do but Valery would be the first to successfully complete the process ahead of time. She knew it was the only way to give her sister back the life she deserved. Mary had been more than kind to postpone her education so she could become employed and begin her livelihood. She was getting ready to open Mary's letter when she heard a light knock on the door.

"Come in." Valery looked up to see her old roommate's face.

"Charlene. Hello. How nice to see you."

"You too. Valery." Valery knew by the look on Charlene's face that something was wrong.

"Now Charlene Wilson, I know you well enough to know when there's something on your mind. What is it.?" Charlene didn't know exactly where to begin. She had always liked Valery and respected her right to be individual and introverted. Valery didn't seem to care that the other girls talked about her because she wouldn't play cards with them on week nights or listen to the sordid intimate details of their boyfriend's experiences. Charlene had learned to play cards and really liked the game of spades even

177

though she had no boyfriend experiences to tell. Whenever girls would have their basement 'hen' sessions, Charlene always made sure she sat at the end of the table and was one of the last ones to talk. She would take bits and pieces of the other girl's experiences and make her story the best. There would be lots of "oohs" and "aahs" when she told her stories. She belly laughed when she got back to her room since none of her made-up flings were true.

Valery never did fraternize with the girls but now she had been seen more than once with one of the new recruits who was ruggedly handsome. Some girls wondered if they were related but one only had to look at Valery's eyes to see the relationship was more than casual. Charlene was all right until some of the girls, who were obviously jealous of what was going on between Valery and John-Claude began saying unscrupulous things about her. It angered Charlene. They had been very close as former roommates and she didn't believe Valery was capable of their ridiculous accusations.

"Well, if you insist." She cleared her throat and began to speak. "We've been noticing you and one of the new soldiers walking around together for the past few weeks. Certain nosy people are wondering how the two of you got so chummy. I know it's none of their business and really it's none of mine, but I now you and..." Valery looked at her old roommate for a moment and then decided that it really didn't matter what was being said. She had no intention of dignifying any of their gossip, but she would tell Charlene how they knew each other.

"I met John-Claude on my first trip to Blue Keyes State College. Although I didn't know him, we were both from New York. His military bus broke down and the recruits were transferred to our bus. There was a vacant seat across from me and he sat in it. He had been drafted by Selective Services to military duty. We talked until the bus got to Norfolk, Virginia.

"Did you all exchange information and write each other?" Charlene realized now that it all made sense.

"No. Once we departed at the bus terminal, I continued my ride on another bus to Blue Keyes and he went on to Virginia to begin boot camp. That was two years ago and I hadn't heard from him since.

"Weren't you happy to see him?" Valery admitted that she was.

"I had thought about him from time to time and wondered what had happened to him. We've talked since he's been on campus but that's all. He told me he had been injured in a bomb blast in Guam but luckily had survived." Valery didn't know if there would be a 'relationship' with him because they hadn't talked about one. She didn't even think she was ready for one. She needed to graduate and that was her main goal.

When Valery finished the conversation, Charlene was almost in tears. It was like a fairy tale. Charlene thought it was wonderful and she hugged Valery and wished her good luck. Somehow she had a hunch that Valery had found the man of her dreams even if she didn't know it yet.

"I'm happy for you Valery. I hope you two make it. After all, you've been here three years and to be honest, it's about time."

"About time for what."

"About time for you to go out and have some fun. You hardly ever dance on Fridays when you do come to the gym or go to the movies on Saturdays." Valery defended her position.

"That's because I have more important things to do like studying or researching. Have you forgotten that's what we're here to do?"

"I know that. But all work and no play makes Jack a dull boy. If you stop and think about it, every human being needs to have a social life, at least that's what my philosophy teacher says. Otherwise, we become shut off from the rest of the world and have all kinds of problems." Valery reached for the letter Mary had written her and began unfolding it, half listening as Charlene babbled on about her new love interest. Charlene could sense Valery wanted to be alone.

"Well, I guess I'll be going now. I have to get to work. If I'm late, I'll be docked and Lord knows I can use all the money I can get."

"Thanks for coming by Charlene. But please don't worry about the things that are being said about me. Believe me, I know what I'm doing." She walked Charlene to the door and as she closed it, she wondered if she was trying to convince Charlene or herself. It had been a little more than two weeks since she had last heard from her sister.

38

Mary had been very busy working at Macy's and business had picked up in some areas but consumers could not always find the brands of products and merchandise they wanted. During the war, silk was produced for a variety of purposes. Derived from the Asiatic moth, silk was used for parachutes, powder bags for naval guns, and for women's hosiery. That however, changed when relations between Japan and the United States deteriorated. The nation's supply of the precious resource was seized in early 1940's by the Office of Production Management. Manufacturers replaced silk stockings with nylons setting off a shopping madness. Cigarettes too were being rationed. Mary wrote that Wandean Leftwitz, her co-worker's husband Walter smoked Phillip Morris and on occasion Camel's. When she went to the market to buy his cigarettes, she was told they had none. They had been replaced with two new brands called Marlboro and Rialto. He husband was furious but had no choice. He told her the government should not have gotten into a war if they were not prepared to take care of both the soldiers as well as the men left behind to take care of the women and children. Walter would curse and tell her he'd bet all the rich men who were draft dodgers were still being supplied with their favorite brands of cigarettes. He began drinking more heavily and on more than one occasion would take his frustration out on her and her older children. Mary even worked overtime to fill in for Wandean when Walter had been on a binge and hit her a little too hard. Although she felt sorry for Wandean, she was grateful for the extra money.

As more men were sent to war, women were no longer able to stay at home. There were fewer men to run businesses and in the rural areas, run the farms. By default, women were forced into the workplace. At first it wasn't so bad since Mary had worked at her present job for a little over three years. She had seniority over the new hires who obtained their jobs after her employment at Macy's. She felt secure and rarely asked for special favors from management. It came as a complete surprise to her when the manager called her into her office and reduced her working hours to a part time position. The cut in salary meant that not only would she have to find a more affordable place to live but there would be no extra money to send to Valery.

39

That evening Valery did see John-Claude in the dining hall. He was seated with some of the other soldiers. She acknowledged his smile by nodding her head. At the dinner table, most of the students were talking about their classes, boyfriends, the teachers they liked or disliked, and the upcoming weekend events that would take place on campus. Valery couldn't think about anything but her sister's dilemma and how she could help her. She didn't think about what she was eating and really didn't have much appetite. When she finished, she got up and left the dining hall. She had brought all of the assignments she needed to work on so she could leave the dining hall and go straight to the library. She walked up the sixteen steps to the library and reached for the door when she heard a familiar voice behind her.

"Allow me." She spun around to see John-Claude at her side.

"I didn't hear you. Where did you come from?" She smiled as she realized how engrossed she had been in thought.

"I got up and left the dining hall two minutes before you did. I was standing right outside the door. I guess you didn't see me. You didn't even look my way. I followed you so closely that if you had turned around I would have probably knocked you down. Whatever you were thinking about, it was pretty intense. By the way, I hope it was me." Valery was glad right now that her complexion was dark enough that he couldn't see her blush. She really liked his personality and wondered why he hadn't already found a girlfriend. She decided she wouldn't ask him about that. As if he was reading her mind again, he decided to broach the question.

"I've been meaning to ask you if it's all right for me to hang around you in my spare time. I mean, if you already have somebody or something. I guess I never really thought to ask you. Valery looked over at John-Claude and thought if he had sounded any more pitiful, she would have cried herself. She was very happy to hear those words, but she knew if she got too serious with anyone it might interfere with her studies. She decided to be reserved in her response.

"I don't have a boyfriend and I don't have time for one. I'm going to be graduating in a few months and until then, I really need to spend my time working on my studies and preparing for my final exams. And what about you? I'm sure you met or came in contact with girls in the service that were probably head over hills in love with you. Do you write them or did you just love them and leave them?" As soon as her question left her lips, she realized that the answers were none of her business and that she should not have asked them.

John-Claude knew there were all kinds of rumors that floated around about men in the service. Some of them were true and some weren't. He never thought about it because he wasn't interested in having affairs with women that may have slept with men from all parts of the world. He didn't care if she believed him or not but he was glad that she had asked.

"It was common for some of the soldiers to go into town on the weekends to have fun at the local bars. Sometimes I even went with them but it wasn't to drink, talk to girls, or even go to bed with them. I went with them so I could write about the places I had been and the things I saw. One day I'll write a book about all the things that happened to me. I'm still writing. At night usually before I go to bed I think about all the things that have happened during the day and I jot it down. There's even an entry with the name of a beautiful girl named Valery in it." John-Claude laughed as he grabbed Valery up, whirled her around and before she could say anything she found herself laughing too. He finally put her down making sure she didn't trip or stumble on the icy step. As she slid through his arms to the ground, she wondered if she could stand up and she held onto him to steady herself. John-Claude never stopped staring at her before he spoke.

"There has been no woman in my life. And as they turned back toward the library door, but not before Valery distinctly heard him say, 'until now'.

40

Mary and Jolene spent most of the weekend moving Mary's things to a smaller apartment in Harlem. Harlem was still home. The apartment dwellers who lived there were very personable and offered to keep some of the furniture Mary didn't have room for until arrangements could be made. She didn't have a lot of time to cook and really appreciated her new apartment neighbor, a woman in her sixties, making sandwiches she took to work and bringing a plate of food nearly every evening until she could get her place organized. The apartment was further from her job than before so she had to get up earlier to catch the subway. The first few days were horrible and one day she overslept and didn't get to work until nine fifteen that morning. According to her schedule she should have been there no later than eight forty five. She was lucky though and made it to work just moments before the manager arrived.

"Good morning." All the girls that worked in the lingerie department liked Mary. No one would have ever said a word about her being a little late. Wandean was very grateful to Mary for helping her when she and her husband had difficulties. When she realized Mary was late she signed her in. She prayed Mary would not call in sick and would come in soon so that she would not get in trouble for having done so.

"Good morning Mary. Is everything okay?"

"Yes. I just haven't gotten used to getting up earlier in the morning to catch the subway. Especially since I've been staying up unpacking boxes late every night. I had to comb my hair and put on my make-up on the subway. I've got to punch in. I'll be back in a minute." Wandean whispered softly to Mary.

"I've already done that for you. I also took the liberty of getting today's memo out of your box. The evening shift retailed some of the items that were out on the morning shift. Before you ring up the customer make sure you tell them. The marketing strategy is to try and get customers to buy more merchandise by offering them more sales. The memo also states that at the end of the month all sales clerks that have sold an average of thirty percent more than their average sale will be given a bonus in their weekly check." Mary liked her job and enjoyed helping women find apparel that was right for them. She did not like the idea of telling customers anything that would encourage them to buy clothes in such dire times. She feared when customers realized the clerks were not concerned about them but about making profit for Macy's, they would lose faith. Mary could not conceive of herself being a part of this strategy and planned to tell her manager when she got a break. Wandean felt the same way but she knew that their jobs were expendable and a little income was better than none. Mary could be stubborn at times but Wandean had to make her see that it wasn't worth it.

"Please don't say anything to Miss Sandy. I'm sure she is just doing what she has been told she must do by corporate. You will just make it harder on yourself."

"I don't see how." Mary frowned. "I have all but been fired as it is. I'm down to part time work and have to get up before 5:00 every morning to get ready and make it here on time. I work four hours. At the end of the week, most of my money is spent on the subway buying tokens. You'd think for my loyalty she would at least have spared my job. Wandean looked wistfully at Mary.

"I know how you must feel but please think about not saying anything, Mary. If you leave, I will not have any friends. Everyone knows what a horrible man my husband has been to me and thinks I must be stupid because I stay with him. They also know that I like you and don't care about your color. You are as light as some of them. I tell them they must stop being jealous of your beauty. You are one of God's children too." Mary understood what Wandean was saying but she hated deceiving her customers. Neither was there a guarantee that she would not lose her job anyway. It seemed that more people and women in particular were applying for jobs each day. On some days, the Office of Employment at Macy's would be lined with people of all races. Some were trying to get custodial position others as store clerks, and some tried to talk their way into getting jobs that didn't even exist.

41

Over the next two months, John-Claude and Valery became inseparable. They were seen everywhere together. They would study together in the library and he would walk her to her classes. Many of the other girls wondered what it was John-Claude saw in her. He could have had his pick from a bevy of beauties yet he chose Valery Lewis. She not only attracted his attention, she possessed an inner beauty that transcended the realm of her skin color. She had bared her soul to him. He came to know her passions, her desires, her strengths, and her weaknesses. He wasn't sure he wanted to admit it but he was in love with Valery. She was the woman he one day intended to marry. She would make a wonderful mother for his children. She was shy, yet there was a boldness about her that one could sense. She was a delightful person and everyone on campus began to respect her for who she was instead of how she looked.

Just as Professor Brown suggested, Valery stayed in contact with her advisor so that she could file the right forms and not be held up for her graduation. Graduation Form 1 had been sent and approved the previous semester. Graduation Form 2 was sent and approved at the beginning of the spring semester. Graduation Form 3 would be sent at the end of the spring semester and the last graduation form would be approved when she had finished all of her course work and had passed her final exams. John-Claude was doing well in all of his classes and would be graduating with Valery's class. He was being trained to operate telecommunications that would send messages to and from large navy vessels with little or no chance of espionage. He had made A's and was allowed to take a few electives of his choice. He had chosen to take chemistry as an elective since Valery was taking the same class too.

Valery had been offered work study in the chemistry lab as a tutor. Since she had been tutored by Dwight, she knew how helpful it had been to have someone to help you understand the formulas and mix them properly. She really liked helping John-Claude. He caught on quickly and before long she would name a property and he would recite the formula. It became a game to them and on some evenings, the custodian would have to ask them to leave the building so he could lock up. Valery thought John-Claude was ready to begin elementary experiments. He was excited because it had been something that he had always wanted to do. She would start him out on simple experiments. The two of them spent hours in the lab working on different formulas. She was thankful that Professor Brown had suggested she receive tutoring in chemistry. The tutor she had worked with was one of the best. He had graduated last spring and had become a pastor. She wasn't sure that he was really interested in the gospel but he was determined that if he was drafted, he'd go in as a chaplain and never have to worry about being on the front lines.

42

It was nearing the middle of the semester when Valery realized she had not received confirmation from her advisor of her pending graduation. Dr. Paul Davis was not an easy man to get along with but he had been assigned as her advisor when Professor Brown left Blue Keyes State. He was a coach, advisor and had been promoted to head of the Physical Education department. Rumor had it that if your complexion was not light enough, your grades would have to be exemplary. That morning, she put her fears aside and decided to go by his office to talk to him. She walked quickly from her dorm to the Physical Education building pulling the hood of her coat closely around her ears. Once inside, she walked toward his secretary's desk. She approached her with a warm smile though the secretary looked quite upset.

"Good morning. I was wondering if it would be possible for me to speak to Dr. Davis." The secretary looked as if she could have burst into tears at any moment. Without saying a word to Valery, she got up from her chair and tapped lightly on his door. She barely opened it and spoke meekly.

"There's a student here to see you."

"Who is it?" His voice sounded cold and without expression. Before he could say another word, Valery walked past the secretary and into his office. Dr. Davis was sitting behind his desk looking at a chess board. He never took his eyes from the board to even acknowledge her presence. He had grown accustomed to playing chess alone and enjoyed doing so. He believed great men should play the game. Matching wits to see which mind would win the war and ultimately render the king useless. He was getting close to a checkmate and really didn't want to stop playing. She cleared her throat and spoke gently.

"Good Morning Dr. Davis. I won't take much of your time but I did want to meet with you to confirm my August graduation. I also need to pick up my comprehension materials and ask you a few questions." Dr. Davis acted as if he hadn't heard a word Valery said and continued to look at the chessboard that seemed to have claimed his utmost attention. She waited for what seemed like an eternity before he looked up from his desk. His response shook her soul.

"Miss Lewis, after looking over your transcript last week, I found several courses that you have not taken that you will need before you can graduate. I certainly don't see any possibility of you doing so by the end of the summer." He handed her a copy of her transcript. Valery did not trust this man and she knew he would do nothing to help her if her course work was not complete.

"I beg your pardon, sir, according to the 1941 Blue Keyes State College catalog that I came in under, I have met all of the stated requirements. The transcript that you have does not include the courses I have taken during any of the summer sessions. I have a copy of my complete transcript with me. I have the Institute seal on it to show its authenticity." Without him having to ask her, she automatically handed him the transcript and sat in the first chair she spotted. He looked nonchalantly at Valery but roughly took the papers from her hands. She tried desperately to hide how helpless and anxious his crass attitude made her feel but she didn't look away from him. He took his time reaching into the pocket of his shirt to retrieve his spectacles as she sat upright in the chair. He frowned for a moment and commented that he didn't know she had taken classes in the summer of 1941. Valery finally felt her shoulders relax a bit as she looked at him and carefully responded.

"Professor Cole Brown was my advisor then." She immediately realized her comment was not well received. Without saying anything else to Valery, he picked up a packet from his desk and handed it to her. He didn't bother explaining any of its contents other any saying the test would be taken in July and the results would be posted as to whether or not she passed or failed. It was the first time she had seen even the slightest hint of a smile come across his face. She got up quickly and started to the door. As she turned the knob to leave, she looked at the man that would administer the four hour long test to her. She wondered if her mentioning Professor Brown's name would come back to haunt her.

43

Paul Davis had always been a man who knew where he was going and how he would get there. When he was a young boy, he remembered playing in his front yard in Columbus, Ohio, where he was born and raised. He was an only child whose mother was over protective. His father never said much and simply let her make all the decisions. She decided what her son ate, when he would go to bed, and who he could play with outdoors. Most of the children in the neighborhood weren't good enough for her little Paul and therefore, he learned at an early age to ignore the children who walked by and waved at him as he swung higher and higher on his swings and slide down his slide. The only children allowed to come and play with him were two other girls whose parents were of the same social background as his parents. They chatted at their wooden fence when they hung clothes on the line at the same time. They walked their children to the nearby school and brought hot lunches to them. They never shared their lunches with the other children because their parents had indoctrinated in them they would pick up germs that could cause them to die. Paul was thoroughly convinced that people who were poor or dark or ugly were malignant creatures to be avoided. Although it was never directly uttered it was inferred their rights were different from people who had more money or were lighter skinned and visually attractive. He grew up thinking he had a responsibility to help make sure the world was not overcome with people of lesser means. It didn't mean that these people deserved nothing but it did mean they didn't deserve as much.

After graduating from high school, Paul became interested in athletics and landed a college scholarship that developed him into a model teacher and prospective college coach. His good looks and his mother's connections really paid off. He was offered a job at Blue Keyes State College in the Athletic Department in the late 1930's and built his reputation, becoming a great asset to the college. President Lee was thrilled to have him as a part of the staff. He quickly established himself with the faculty there and was known as one of Dr. Lee's 'boys' behind closed doors.

Paul Davis took his job very seriously and he learned to not only consider a student's scholarliness but also their ability to get the job done on the field. He always remembered what his mother told him about how some people were 'all brawn and no brains'. He worked to help students find mentors if needed, adjust to college life, and offered them advice while making sure he produced winning teams. It had taken him five years to finally get rid of Dr. Bobbie Clark, the acting Head of the Athletic Department. He knew he would, but he had to take his time. It was not a secret on campus that Dr. Clark had a drinking problem. It was no wonder since he had been a star athlete at one point in his life. Dr. Clark knew he should have made it to the big leagues but Negroes in that day had little chance if any. He resented having been thrust aside because of his race. Eventually his drinking became so obsessive that he confided in his colleague Paul Davis that he needed help. And that's what he got. Dr. Davis helped him right out of his job when he documented and reported his drinking binges to President Lee. It would be a breeze from then on. Paul Davis met with the president consistently, informing him of the whereabouts of Dr. Clark and planned his ultimate demise. Paul thought the set up was simple and well executed. He would invite him out for drinks the night before the last football game of the year being that it was the most important one. It was homecoming and Dr. Clark accepted the invitation knowing Paul would be discreet in procuring a place with no chance of him running into any of his own players. All the players knew what homecoming meant to the school. They were dedicated and had every intention of making Blue Keyes State the talk of the town.

That evening, Paul Davis dressed modestly in his white shirt and black trousers. He drove his Ford in front of Bobbie Clark's cottage and blew the horn. Dr. Clark came out quickly.

"How goes it man?" Paul could tell right away that Bobbie had already been drinking. This would be easier than he had hoped. He had already phoned President Lee and told him he had overheard Dr. Clark making plans to go out for the evening. He also threw in the lie that some of the boys had rumored Dr. Clark would be meeting one of the cheerleaders there and was planning to have a real good time. President Lee was enraged and wanted to go to his cottage and fire him on the spot. It was Paul Davis who convinced him it would be much more effective if he were caught in the act.

It was nine thirty and the evening looked promising when Bobbie Clark and Paul Davis pulled up to the Red Light Inn. It had been named so because outside the door was a red light that signaled it was the type of establishment that allowed questionable activities. Above the one room club were four small rooms used for more private matters.

Paul let Bobbie out at the front door and told him he would park the car. He had no intention of going inside the Red Light Inn. He knew drunks and they never needed anyone to be with them to have a good time. Professor Clark was already known by the local townspeople and when he entered the door, he was greeted with handshakes and slaps on the back. One man that he didn't even know quickly offered him a drink. From experience, Bobbie knew all he had to do was start talking about the team, the play, his life as a well-known former football standout, and occasionally listen to someone else talk, and he'd never have to pay for a drink. For several hours, the drinks kept coming. By midnight, Bobbie was so inebriated, it had taken two surly men to help him up the stairs where he lay sprawled out on the bed. When the President arrived at the Inn, he was taken to the upstairs bedroom where Bobbie lay snoring peacefully. The scene sickened him. Needing no more evidence, he left the Red Light Inn, promptly returned to his office and wrote a letter to Dr. Bobbie Clark informing him of his immediate dismissal.

Paul Davis returned to the Inn to pick up the Professor around three o'clock that morning. He helped Bobbie get dressed and paid the waitress an extra twenty bucks to keep her mouth shut. He drove the two of them back to the campus and let him out at his cottage. By nine o'clock the letter written by President Lee was delivered to Dr. Bobbie Clark informing him that he was no longer an employee of Blue Keyes State College. The letter instructed him that he had twenty four hours to get off the campus or he would be arrested. The next day, Paul Davis smiled as he watched the car of Bobbie Clark slowly drive toward the college entrance to exit the grounds escorted by campus security. He had checkmated his opponent. After several meetings and hearings with the President, board of Directors, and members of the Physical Education Committee, Dr. Paul Davis was named head of the Physical Education Department at Blue Keyes State College. It took him a year to adjust to the accolades that went along with his new position, but after a while he became somewhat iconic.

As time went on, Paul Davis' colleagues began noticing significant changes in his behavior. He became more demanding in the workload and added their names to additional committees whether they consented or not. Whenever instructors complained, their contract was not extended to them the next year. Athletic scholarships were awarded to students based on who they were, what they looked like and how nice they were to him. He held private interviews with all students that were interested in being a physical education major. Most of the physical education majors were nicely built, having spent most of their time keeping in shape during high school. Some students were interested in the health aspect of physical education but if not extremely intelligent or attractive, they were told there was no more scholarship money available. They were however, always encouraged to apply the following year. There were no exceptions. Everyone had to come by him.

Valery Lewis had been quite brazen to come into his office demanding her way to see him. She even had the audacity to insinuate his incompetence. Few people had ever gone that far with him. He looked at the transcript in front of him once again. After setting up his chess board, he picked up the phone and placed a call to New York. The game began.

44

The atmosphere of Blue Keyes had changed quite a bit since the arrival of the soldiers. The young ladies weren't in as much competition for attention from males and it seemed as if even the fraternities and sororities tolerated each other. Harassing pledgees was a normal occurrence on campus with everyone in full swing. Vera, a girl who lived down the hall on the second floor had chosen to become Greek. She was told she needed to fill one of the bathtubs on the first floor with water. Vera didn't think the request was too much to ask until she was presented with a thimble. Her exact instructions were to fill the thimble with water and pour the thimble full of water into the tub until the tub was full. At first, Vera thought her big sister would let her do it for a while and then let her stop, but after several hours passed, the bottom of the tub was barely full. She had missed all of her classes yet her temperament was still cheerful. Valery had seen her earlier and thought it an odd thing for a pledgee to do but she didn't comment. It was really none of her business. Charlene was visiting Valery that day. Having become rather rambunctious in her days of maturing she thought she'd help Vera out at no cost. Each time Vera put a thimble full of water in the tub and went back upstairs to get another, Charlene would turn the water on and fill the tub full of water. Each time the big sisters would come back to check the pledgee's progress, they would see the tub full, make her empty it out, and start over again.

Valery knew she would never be Greek. She felt if one could be treated that badly by people that were supposed to care about you, she'd really hate to see them dislike her. For that reason, she chose to remain uncommitted. She had found someone that made her happy and perhaps one day she and John-Claude would have a very special relationship. He had proven to be someone she could rely on and talk to about anything. He knew everything about her. She remembered the day she told him about her parents' accident. He listened somberly as she spoke and when she finished, he held her a long time. He knew her feelings about the whole situation had her tied in an emotional knot. She was really obsessed about finishing school quickly and going back to New York to give her sister a chance to finish her education. He really wished he could just change the way she blamed herself for everything all the time. He had secretly decided to ask for her hand in marriage when the opportunity presented itself.

45

Valery Lewis had no idea she had become a target of a small cadre of upper echelon administrators. She went along placidly working on her studies and preparing for her graduation. The spring weather brought its usual temperamental changes. Most of the snow had left the mountainside as the trees began to blossom and the sap rose. Valery could feel the end of the spring semester coming and it gave her such delight. The campus seemed to be awakening from its winter sleep as more students lingered on the outside laughing and talking. She and John-Claude had agreed to meet for lunch and afterwards head to the library. Once inside the cafeteria, they decided to sit near the freshman tables. They were serving roast beef, mashed potatoes, turnip greens, yams, and hot rolls. The savory smells were tantalizing and Valery knew she was really going to enjoy the meal. After the grace was sung, they waited for the platters of food to come around so they could serve themselves. It was still customary for freshmen to get the leftovers and she had almost forgotten how cruel her fellow upperclassmen could be. At their table, two freshman girls came into the dining hall late and couldn't find a seat at a table designated for freshman. They saw two vacant seats at the table where John-Claude and Valery sat. Valery had seen them before but didn't know their names. The food had already been passed around and one of the girls looked over at Charles Stone, the loudmouthed senior who tried to embarrass anyone he could for no reason. One of the girls spoke to him.

"Could you pass the salad please?" Charles looked on the table for a moment then darted his eyes back and forth from one platter to the other.

"The salad? What salad? There's no salad on the table." The girl looked as though she was in no mood for his antics. She asked again.

"Pass the salad, please." This time Charles was determined to get a little mileage out of her unfortunate lack of correct terminology at least in his opinion. He stood up and encircled his body as he rocked and reeled from left to right looking as if there was some mystery to be solved.

"If anyone sees any salad on their table please pass it over here." It was obvious the girl who had come in didn't realized that her reference to salad was really a request for the turnip greens. Charles also realized that he had a small audience and he was going to seize the moment. With an air of sophistication, Charles strolled to the head of the table, pointing to each item on the table.

"This is roast beef. These are mashed potatoes, these are turnip greens, these are yams, and these are rolls." He then acted as though a revelation had come as he pointed to the greens on the table.

"Are you talking about these?" The freshman both visibly embarrassed and angry, glared at him silently.

"Well, my dear, this is not salad, these are greens. Salad is usually a mixture of lettuce, tomatoes, and cucumbers, serve with some type of dressing. Now, do you want the greens?" Charles had always gotten the last laugh and today was no different. The girl however, had grown up with a family of boys and was used to fighting with them and for the most part winning. She had heard of Charles but never thought that she'd have a confrontation with him. She knew she had two choices. Either fight him or be the laughing stock of the campus for a least one day. She decided to fight. The girl with her whispered desperately in her ear pleading with her to just leave. Though furious, she stood up and walked out of the dining hall without touching her food, her friend walking closely behind her. When the two got outside, once again, the girl's friend pled with her not to wait for Charles to come outside the dining hall so she could fight him. At the moment, she knew she would get kicked out of school but she didn't care.

Valery and John-Claude, who had witnessed the entire debacle got up from the table and even though they said nothing, it was obvious neither of them were pleased with Charles' assault on the innocent freshman. They talked about the incident on their way to the library. Charles' behavior reminded John-Claude a little of his old friend Kape.

"People that come from different parts of the country have different meanings for things they say." John-Claude hated to think Charles really understood how hurtful it must have been to the young lady but Valery wasn't budging on her stance.

"Charles knew exactly what she meant when she asked for the 'salad' the first time. Maybe he didn't get a lot of attention when he was young so now he gets it any way he can. Have you noticed one girl following around after him? But how could anybody be attracted to someone like that? Why don't you have a word with him?" Valery looked at John-Claude teasingly. John-Claude waved his hands back and forth.

"No ma'am. I'm not about to give up one moment of my time talking to mouth-all-mighty, Charles Stone. No thank you." Valery tried to keep a straight face as long as she could before bursting into laughter. John-Claude loved it when she laughed that way. He stopped and looked into her eyes. When Valery laughed, the sun shined a little brighter and for a moment he thought he would ask her to be his wife right then, but hesitated. It was then that he realized the perfect moment would be the day she walked across the stage and received her diploma. He knew how much graduation meant to her and he wouldn't stand in her way.

Valery and John-Claude worked in the library until late that evening and she was finally glad to get to her room. She was exhausted and fell asleep right after she bathed, put on her pajamas and said her prayers. She slept soundly through the night.

46

Over the next few weeks, Valery began to see less of John-Claude spending much of her time preparing for her final examinations. When the day arrived, she felt strong and was ready as she and her peers filed quietly into the testing examination room. She had sat near the front and waited anxiously as the proctors passed out the test booklets and the required number two pencils.

"Good morning students…" The timed test lasts for a full four hours with only one break. She was mentally drained but when it was over, she was confident she had met the needed criteria to graduate. She met John-Claude afterwards. They decided to skip lunch and go for a walk. She needed to clear her head.

"Well, how do you feel?" John-Claude was glad that ordeal was over for the both of them. Now she could relax and he could spend the time with her he had been craving.

"I feel relieved I think. I can't wait to tell Mary. She said she was looking forward to coming to the graduation. Jolene and the Brown's are coming too. Valery suddenly realized she was starved.

"Let's eat."

47

Paul Davis had made several calls to New York. He had exhausted most of his resources when he finally received some information that peaked his interest. It seemed that a young lady named Valery Lewis had lost her parents in a tragic car accident. Police records revealed that the accident had occurred when the parents were delivering a paper to the school for a daughter named Valery. The daughter had given a sworn statement that corroborated her parents were on their way to school to deliver some school paper she'd left at home and were T-boned when a transfer truck ran a red light.

Dr. Davis normally wouldn't have gone to such lengths to interrogate a student, but for some reason he felt he needed to teach her a lesson she'd never forget. She had been too haughty the day she had come to his office. Every now and then it was good to make an example out of a student that would keep the others at bay. This young lady had good grades however the final exams were sometimes tricky at best. He had the final say on actual test scores and knew how to manipulate them. After the committee recommended the grades, he was always at some point left to review and change final scores if he deemed it necessary. He also was responsible for posting the identification numbers of students that would be graduating. According to procedure, any student could contest the score, but it never did any good, since students were not able to see their actual tests again or the answer key that provided all correct answers. Besides that, the oral parts of the exam were subjectively graded. It all boiled down to whether the department decided to let you graduate based on their criteria.

The information Dr. Davis had in his possession had come from the son of a friend and very bright attorney who had formerly served in the army. It was rumored he had not done well in the military and had decided to practice law in New York. He had met Paul Davis through a mutual friend. Paul and lawyer Ronnie Kapeheart had a lot in common. They were both the same age. Neither were married and both were unscrupulous. Ronnie had been instrumental in helping Paul plan the demise of the former physical education department head. When Ronnie found out that John-Claude had ended up there, he was even more determined to keep up with Blue Keyes State. It had been coincidental that Ronnie found out that John-Claude Adams was there. Paul had illegally mailed him a copy of the ASTP men on campus. Kape had never forgotten the night he was caught and punished for falling asleep while on guard duty at Fort Story while John-Claude went free. He too, remembered how his plot to return the favor had almost cost John-Claude his life. Kape blamed John-Claude for his dishonorable discharge from the military. Luckily, his father was able to save his career.

Ronnie Kapeheart never meant for anything to happen to John-Claude but that was beside the point. They had all been lucky just to be alive. Through their communication, Kape also found out that the young woman who Paul was interrogating was also the college sweetheart of his old war buddy. Information concerning a sister named Mary was also in the report. Kape traced her whereabouts to a less than pristine apartment building in Harlem. The report noted that she had once been a student at NYU, majoring in law. Her grades were excellent but for some reason she dropped out. Dr. Davis surmised by noting the age difference in the two girls pointed to the fact that the older sister likely left school and got a job to support the younger sister. Paul Davis was thrilled. He had all the ammunition he needed. Before he ended the conversation with Kape, he invited him to come to the campus and enjoy the sites. He assured him since it was almost time for summer graduation, there would be lots of faculty parties to attend. Kape had been around enough college campuses to know exactly what he meant. The two men replaced their telephones on their hooks. It was time for Paul Davis to act on his plan.

48

One week before graduation, final examination scores were posted. Everyone was crowded around the outside of the physical education department door. Students were nervously and frantically searching for their identification numbers, searching for the word 'passed' that would set their minds free from the impact the pending scores would have on their future. Valery had gone without John-Claude, too nervous to control her thoughts but he was already there waiting for her and searching for his notification.

"I knew you'd be here. Have you seen your scores? Valery smiled and he hugged her.

"Congratulations. Let's celebrate." John-Claude, at a loss for words himself, could understand why Valery could hardly speak.

"I'll catch you later. I'm meeting Charlene and her roommate." John-Claude winked at her as she hurried to meet her friends. Deep inside, Valery knew she had a score to settle.

49

Paul Davis felt he had been patience yet, Valery Lewis had gone too far when she wrote the letter of complaint against him to President Lee. She had also written letters to former teachers who shared letters of recommendation as to her character and her studiousness. When the President summoned Paul, he was warned to be careful with the Lewis girl. Dr. Lee reminded him that it would not look good for Blue Keyes State if word got out that the school made differences in the students based on their looks or their color. The president also had a copy of Valery Lewis's transcript with hm. He went over her grades with the professor pointing out the likelihood she would not have failed under normal circumstances.

"What's really going on with this girl, Paul?"

"It's very simple sir. The young lady has probably spent too much time running around with one of the ASTP recruits and didn't spend enough time getting prepared for her comprehensive exams." Paul Davis attempted to look sincere when he talked to the president but there was obviously something very wrong.

"I know it has been a tradition at Blue Keyes State that we highlight certain students because of their background or exposure but we must make certain students from less affluent backgrounds get a chance to do well. It there is some..." Paul Davis responded before the president could finish his sentence.

"No, President Lee. I have no ulterior motive on this one sir. I'm simply doing my best to make sure all graduates leaving Blue Keyes State College are qualified to represent this college well. If you would like me to illegally give Miss Lewis a passing grade."

"Why of course not!" President Lee could tell Paul was beginning to feel a bit edgy.

"Very well. That will be all Dr. Davis." The two stood, shook hands, and Paul Davis walked out. Just outside the president's office he was exhilarated by the fact he knew Dr. Lee would succumb to his terms. Although Valery Lewis had done her best to expose him, she had failed. It took exactly ten minutes for him to stride from the president's office back to his. He immediately called his secretary into his office to type a letter and hand deliver it to Miss Lewis.

50

Valery locked the door to her room and decided to stop by the dorm matron's office to check on her mail. She spotted the secretary who she remembered was sitting at a desk just outside Professor Davis' outer office when she visited him. She approached Valery nervously.

"Miss Valery Lewis?"

"Yes. I'm Valery Lewis." The secretary cleared her throat.

"I have been told that I must personally deliver this letter to you." Valery braved a smile.

"Good news I hope."

"I hope so too. Goodbye."

"Wait…" Valery wanted to ask her some questions but the secretary almost ran out of the building headed back to the physical education building. Valery quickly tore open the letter and read its contents.

Dear Miss Lewis,

> It has come to my attention that there are some concerns as to the legitimacy of the graduate scores you received on July 24, 1944. I assure you every possible effort was made to accommodate each student that was eligible to take the Graduate Comprehensive Exam. I would like to go over

any details or concerns you may have. If an error has been made, we are ready to make the necessary concessions. I am scheduling a conference with you on Wednesday, July 26, 1944.

Professor Paul Davis

P.E. Department Chair

The letter didn't tell her much but it gave her something to think about. Perhaps he had thought about how unfairly she had been treated and wanted to make amends. If she didn't pass, she just didn't pass, but she knew that her knowledge far surpassed at least two other girls, yet they were going to graduate. She would plead with him and continue to contest the unfairness of the scores, but she would never consider doing what the other girls unabashedly let be known had done to get their grades changed. At any rate, she would have her day on tomorrow.

That evening she met John-Claude for supper. She wasn't hungry at all but she made herself eat knowing that she must keep her strength. Since the war was in full swing, it was rumored that the stringy beef-like protein they were being served was actually horse meat. Valery tried not to think about it as she consumed her meal. Afterwards, she and John-Claude left the dining hall and found a nice quiet place near the library to talk.

"Are you nervous?" John-Claude wasn't really sure that Valery was ready to confront Dr. Davis but she knew it was her only chance.

"Ready as I'll ever be. Two of the girls actually told me they visited Dr. Davis after hours and the next day their grades were changed and their identifications posted as 'passing'. John-Claude clenched his teeth tightly together at the thought of Valery being taken in by Paul Davis' manipulative schemes.

220

"When I confront him, he'll have no recourse but to pass me. I don't want to, but if I have to go to the President again, I will." John-Claude wondered if Valery really thought that Dr. Davis would ever admit to any wrongdoing. He was trying to prepare her for the worse.

"What if he still refuses to change your grade? Are you going to stay here another semester and retake the exams? It really wouldn't be so bad would it? I'd even stay around if you wanted me to." Valery half listened to John-Claude willing herself to believe it would work out in her favor. It had to. It was her only chance. .

51

It was early the next day when Valery arose from her bed before six o'clock to collect her thoughts and get ready for her meeting with Dr. Davis. She decided to skip breakfast and by eight forty five she was waiting for Dr. Davis to see her. He had given his secretary the morning off, leaving the front office vacant. The professor would have no witnesses to whatever transpired between the two of them. At exactly nine o'clock, the door to his office opened and Dr. Davis stood in the doorway. He was wearing black slacks with a yellow Arrow shirt. His black shoes had been shined and he seemed to look taller than ever. Valery forced a smile but his look was stern and unrelenting.

"You may come in." He looked condescendingly at her as she walked past him and occupied the brown leather chair across from his desk. As he closed the door and went to his seat, he thought how she would grovel at his feet, but his mind was made up.

"Miss Lewis, I've decided to have this meeting with you out of common courtesy. President Lee and I have already met and discussed your situation. The required minimum score to graduate as set by the College Board has not been met. We have an obligation to…" Valery listened while he continued to discuss possible reasons for her failures. He then picked up another file marked 'Confidential'. He handed it to her and asked if she recognized the contents. She opened the file and to her horror, pictures of her mother and father taken after their tragic accident fell to the floor. Valery had never seen the pictures and she stared for a long time before her eyes welled with tears. She didn't remember leaving Dr. Davis' office nor running back to her dorm. Sometime later John-Claude came by the dorm and asked the dorm matron to knock on her door.

"Come in." Valery called weakly, as she could find few words to say. Joyce entered her room and spoke gently to her.

"John-Claude is downstairs and wants to see you. What shall I tell him?" Valery couldn't look in her face.

"Tell him I'm not feeling well but I'll see him tomorrow. Thank you for delivering the message." Joyce left the room closing her door softly behind her. Valery slept sporadically that night.

52

The last time Valery looked at the clock it was five forty seven the next morning. She had been awake for hours. Going over the events of the day before disturbed the little bit of sleep she should have gotten. She cut the small lamp that had been a part of her life for the past three years on and swung her legs over to the right side of the bed. She reached in the top drawer where she kept her note paper and pen. It took her about ten minutes to write a note to her sister.

John-Claude was the only one that really understood her and she quickly penned him too. He would perhaps be the least deserving of the tragedy that was to come, yet Valery knew he would understand. He always had. She finished the letters with her usual simple closure of 'Love, Val." She stared at the letters for a long while before she stuffed them under her mattress. She ran her bath water and slowly immersed herself. Today, the water felt just right. It enveloped her as a cloud and at that moment she knew she had made the right choice.

She had taken her time to lay out her attire for the day. She would wear white for the occasion. She sometimes wondered why she loved to wear the color white. Maybe it was because it was in such contrast to her skin which made her stand out in a crowd. She had not been raised to be ashamed of her skin color. There would one day be a reckoning for those who saw her any differently. Today she would even put on her white scarf. Valery looked long and hard at her body as she delicately towel dried herself. Her tiny waist and curvy hips accentuating her hour glass figure. She slowly rubbed lotion over her supple black skin. She brushed her hair back placing her scarf neatly around the edges of her hairline. Slipping into her white shorts, puffy short white sleeved blouse and white tennis shoes, Valery grabbed her jacket and left the dorm. Her clothes had been packed now for more than two days. With everything taken care of, she felt a sense of relief. She knew that John-Claude would be waiting for her in the dining hall as usual for their breakfast. It had become their routine. Today she had to forego the food that would normally start her day. Today would be different. By eight thirty, the sun was nearly over the tall trees that lined the campus. Valery walked leisurely to the administration building toward the chemistry lab.

53

John-Claude had dreamed of Valery that night. He saw her dressed in a beautiful long white gown coming toward him with her arms outstretched. He was standing there smiling in a black tuxedo waiting for her. Somewhere between them holding hands and being pronounced by the priest as husband and wife, he woke up. He'd thought about Valery for a long time yesterday. He was sorry she had refused to see him. Taking in the news of not have passed her comprehensive exams had hit her hard even though she tried to hide behind a brave smile. He had wanted to comfort her and planned a special surprise he hoped would change her mood. Being unable to sleep any longer, he got up, took his shower and dressed in his military attire. He wanted to look his best when she saw him.

Being late for breakfast was something that was not taken lightly at Blue Keyes State College but today John-Claude intended to be late. He wanted everyone's attention when he presented Valery with her engagement ring. As planned, John-Claude turned many heads as he walked into the dining hall that morning. He strolled to the table which usually was occupied by the woman he intended to make happy for the rest of her life. She was never normally late but it didn't bother him since he knew she would be coming. He poured a glass of orange juice and beckoned for a waited to come.

"Is there any ginger ale in the kitchen?" The waiter nodded and headed for the kitchen and returned with the ginger ale, placing it on the table in front of him. At nine o'clock, John-Claude looked at his watch and wondered if in all the confusion, perhaps they were supposed to meet somewhere else. He realized he obviously must have misunderstood their meeting place. He left the dining hall having touched none of his food. He walked toward the physical education building to try and catch Valery before he went back to his dorm.

54

The security guard was just opening the chemistry lab when Valery arrived. She had been her pleasant, usual self when she greeted Officer Eanes. He had always been such a nice man.

"Good morning, young lady." He was surprised to see anyone coming to the lab so early.

"Got some last minutes lab tests to run?" Valery was quite calm as she looked into his gray eyes etched with years of hard work in them.

"Yes, sir. I've completed all of my course work and forgot to include the results of one test I ran earlier. Would you mind letting me finish it up? I promise not to take too long."

"Oh take your time Miss. I'm in no hurry." Officer Eanes thought Valery was such a delicate student. He knew from her northern accent she wasn't from around the Blue Keyes area. Whenever she came around, he would always try to start up a conversation with her so he could listen to her talk. She talked like she was somebody going somewhere. He had noticed when she began to take up with one of the ASTP fellows. He was a nice young man too. Seemed as if they were always together but they were very respectful. They weren't the type you'd catch behind a bush. Officer Eanes thought a good girl like that would one day make someone a real fine wife. Valery gave him a big smile as she thanked him again for opening the lab and letting her inside.

Once inside, she looked around the room. She needed to take care of this business quickly. Officer Eanes continued to make his rounds through the building, unlocking the doors and checking to make sure the lights were on and all offices were unlocked. The tables in the lab were lined with the normal materials. She would only need three test tubes. The eyedropper and test tubes were easily accessible to her but all chemicals were locked up. Officer Eanes would be fired if it could be proven he opened the door that stored the chemicals but Valery had already thought of that. She had never returned the key that she had been given by Dwight, the tutor Professor Brown assigned to her two years earlier. She would leave the key in the door so that once records were checked, it would prove that it was the key assigned to Dwight and not Officer Eanes' key. Valery walked casually to the door. She opened it and looked down the hallway both ways before she closed the door and quickly turned off the lights. She felt her way back to the first table gingerly sliding her hand across it until it touched what she knew were the test tubes. She removed three of them from their stands and reaching in her shorts pocket, she removed the key that let her inside where dozens of chemicals were lined. It took no more than five minutes for Valery to make the concoction that would make Professor Davis pay for his cruelty to her.

After she had finished, she carefully poured what was commonly known as arsenic into a small vial, slipping it undetectably into her jacket. She closed and locked the chemical storage room and walked over to cut the lights back on. Officer Eanes had made his rounds and was on his way back down the hall when he opened the door to check on her. She was rinsing the test tubes out when he called to her.

"Bout done there, little lady?" She looked at him and smiled.

"All done here." Valery replaced the test tubes back on their stands, picked up her notebook and left.

55

By the time John-Claude reached the physical education building, most of the students he knew were leaving the building. He went inside and looked around. There was no sign of her there but he thought she might be in the gym exercising or running laps to take the edge off her frayed nerves. Lois Wade, met him as he walked onto the gym floor.

"Hello handsome."

"Hi Lois. Tell me you have seen my future bride and make me a happy man."

"I'll tell you anything you want to hear." Lois moved closer to John-Claude hoping to evoke a favorable response.

"Now behave yourself Lois. You know that it would be a shame for your boyfriend or should I say boyfriends to find out that you flirt with other men." Lois bristled at John-Claude and rolled her eyes at him as she walked away.

"No. I haven't seen your precious pet. As a matter of fact, she hasn't been here today." John-Claude thought for a moment and decided that he would go to her dorm to find out if she had gotten sick or perhaps had gone to the infirmary. He knew that although Valery was a strong person, she was still very fragile in some ways. Her pride had been bruised and he wanted to be with her as much as possible until she could get over the shock of not being able to graduate as she had planned. He also knew that it was possible that she may have gone back once again to try and reason with Dr. Davis in his office. He checked the infirmary but she had not been there either. He went back to her dormitory but no one had seen her leave. He then went to Dr. Davis' office but his secretary said Valery had not been seen there either.

56

When Valery finally reached the library, she swung the door open and entered. Her steps felt labored as she walked methodically to the second floor of the building. It had always been her favorite place. It was the place where she and John-Claude had talked for numerous hours about everything and nothing. It was the room in which she had first held hands with him and the table where she had written many letters to Mary and Jolene, and the Browns. It was where she had prayed for strength for herself to ease the guilt that had never completely left her soul. This was a time in her life that should have been stored with happy memories of her college days but instead it had come to a standstill.

Valery reached her hand into her shorts pocket and pulled out the small vial of arsenic she had carried around with her for the last hour. She took the top off quickly and leaned her head back as she downed its contents. She got up and walked down the stairs to the first floor. She went to the reference section of the library and picked up the New York Times before she found a comfortable seat. Valery knew it wouldn't take long for the chemicals to take effect. She read the paper trying to remember as much as she could before she slipped away. She could feel her eyelids closing and did nothing to try and stop them. She welcomed the sleep that was enveloping her like a cloud rising to meet the sky. She felt at ease now. There was someone calling her but she could not answer.

Epilogue

An emergency assembly was called for the entire student body of Blue Keyes State College. The President already had his speech which was eloquent and to the point. He knew the students would be in no mood for conversation. He also knew he had to protect himself from the harsh criticism that was sure to some from the students, the community, and the local press. President Lee promised he would do all in his power to help them get over the loss of one of their own. John-Claude had been in attendance yet he barely heard a word the president said. He could only think about her. Why had she done this? Was there more that she had not told him? He wanted to talk to Paul Davis. He wanted answers but in the meantime, he wanted the world to know the truth.

Every day, for two weeks after her death, notes were placed beneath the doors of the student's dorm rooms telling everyone what color clothing would be worn. During vespers there was total silence with no one applauding for the presidents' speeches.

Among the things Valery left behind were two notes. One was written to John-Claude telling him of her love for him. Valery requested that her body be buried behind Dr. Davis' office between the two large pine trees that could be seen through his office windows. She wanted him to remember her. Mary Lewis tucked her letter away in her purse. Valery's body was taken back to New York, where she was buried in a small unmarked grave. At last Valery was free.

It was 1945, the war had ended, and Blue Keyes State College began the fall semester with the new freshmen standing in line waiting to register for the new academic year. The new student body president looked forward to the freshmen initiation of black beanies and dog tags.